F. Anstey

Voces Populi

Second Edition

F. Anstey

Voces Populi
Second Edition

ISBN/EAN: 9783337249120

Printed in Europe, USA, Canada, Australia, Japan

Cover: Foto ©Andreas Hilbeck / pixelio.de

More available books at **www.hansebooks.com**

VOCES POPULI

FEMALE ARTISTE (SINGS REFRAIN).

VOCES POPULI

[Reprinted from " Punch "]

BY

F. ANSTEY

AUTHOR OF "VICE VERSÂ," ETC.

SECOND SERIES

WITH TWENTY-FIVE ILLUSTRATIONS

BY J. BERNARD PARTRIDGE

SECOND EDITION

LONDON

LONGMANS, GREEN, AND CO.

AND NEW YORK: 15 EAST 16th STREET

1892

CONTENTS

ILLUSTRATIONS

VOCES POPULI

An Evening with a Conjuror.

SCENE—*A Suburban Hall. The Performance has not yet begun. The Audience is limited and low-spirited, and may perhaps number—including the Attendants—eighteen. The only people in the front seats are a man in full evening dress, which he tries to conceal under a caped coat, and two Ladies in plush opera-cloaks. Fog is hanging about in the rafters, and the gas-stars sing a melancholy dirge. Each casual cough arouses dismal echoes. Enter an intending Spectator, who is conducted to a seat in the middle of an empty row. After removing his hat and coat, he suddenly thinks better—or worse—of it, puts them on again, and vanishes hurriedly.*

FIRST SARDONIC ATTENDANT (*at doorway*). Reg'lar turnin' em away to-night, *we* are !

SECOND SARDONIC ATTENDANT. He come up to me afore he goes to the pay-box, and sez he—"Is there a seat left ?" he sez. And I sez to 'im, "Well, I *think* we can manage to squeeze you in somewhere." Like that, I sez.

> [*The Orchestra, consisting of two thin-armed little girls, with pigtails, enter, and perform a stumbling Overture upon a cracked piano.* HERR VON KAMBERWOIL, *the Conjuror, appears on platform, amidst loud clapping from two obvious Confederates in a back row.*

HERR V. K. (*in a mixed accent*). Lyties and Shentilmans, pefoor I co-mence viz my hillusions zis hevenin' I 'ave most hemphadically to repoodiate hall assistance from hany spirrids or soopernatural beins vatsohever. All I shall 'ave ze honour of showing you will be perform by simple Sloight of 'and or Ledger-dee-Mang! (*He invites any member of the Audience to step up and assist him, but the spectators remain coy.*) I see zat I 'ave not to night so larsh an orjence to select from as usual, still I 'ope—(*Here one of the obvious Confederates slouches up, and joins him on the platform.*) Ah, zat is goot! I am vair much oblige to you, Sare. (*The Confederate grins sheepishly.*) Led me see—I seem to remember your face some'ow. (*Broader grin from Confederate.*) Hah you vos 'ere last night?—zat exblains it! But you 'ave nevaire assist me befoor, eh? (*Reckless shake of the head from Confederate.*) I thought nod. *Vair* vell. You 'ave nevaire done any dricks mit carts—no? Bot you will dry? You never dell vat you gan do till you dry, as ze ole sow said ven she learn ze halphabet. (*He pauses for a laugh—which doesn't come.*) Now, Sare, you know a cart ven you see 'im? Ah, zat is somtings alretty! Now I vill ask you to choose any cart or carts out of zis back. (*The Confederate fumbles.*) I don't vish to 'urry you—but I vant you to mike 'aste—&c., &c.

THE MAN IN EVENING DRESS. I remember giving Bimbo, the Wizard of the West, a guinea once to teach me that trick—there was nothing in it.

FIRST LADY IN PLUSH CLOAK. And can you *do* it?

THE M. IN E. D. (*guardedly*). Well, I don't know that I could exactly do it *now*—but I know how it's done.

[*He explains elaborately how it is done.*

HERR V. K. (*stamping, as a signal that the Orchestra may leave off*). Next I shall show you my zelebrated hillusion of ze inexhaustible 'At, to gonclude viz the Invisible 'En. And I shall be moch oblige if any shentilmans vill kindly favour me viz 'is 'at for ze purpose of my exberiment.

THE M. IN E. D. Here's mine—it's quite at your service. [*To his companions.*] This is a stale old trick, he merely—(*explains as before*). But you wait and see how I'll score off him over it!

"LED ME SEE—I SEEM TO REMEMBER YOUR FACE SOME'OW."

HERR V. K. (*to the* M. in E. D.). You are gvide sure, Sare, you leaf nossing insoide of your 'at ?

THE M. IN E. D. (*with a wink to his neighbours*). On the contrary, there are several little things there belonging to me, which I'll thank you to give me back by-and-by.

HERR V. K. (*diving into the hat*). So? Vat 'ave we 'ere? A bonch of flowairs! Anozzer bonch of flowairs? Anozzer—*and* anozzer! IIa, do you alvays garry flowairs insoide your 'at, Sare?

THE M. IN E. D. Invariably—to keep my head cool ; so hand them over, please ; I want them.

[*His Companions titter, and declare " it really is* too *bad of him !* "

HERR V. K. Bresently, Sare,—zere is somtings ailse, it feels loike—yes, it ees—a mahouse-drap. Your haid is drouble vid moice, Sare, yes? Bot zere is none 'ere in ze 'at !

THE M. IN E. D. (*with rather feeble indignation*). I never said there were.

HERR V. K. No, zere is no mahouse—bot—[*diving again*]—ha ! a leedle vide rad ! Anozzer vide rad ! And again a vide rad—and one, two, dree *more* vide rads ! You vind zey keep your haid noice and cool, Sare? May I drouble you to com and dake zem avay? I don't loike the vide rads myself, it is madder of daste. [*The Audience snigger.*] Oh, bot vait—zis is a *most* gonvenient 'at—[*extracting a large feeding-bottle and a complete set of baby-linen*]—ze shentelman is vairy domestic I see. And zere is more yet, he is goot business man, he knows ow von must hadvertise in zese' ere toimes. 'E 'as 'elp me, so I vill 'elp 'im by distributing some of his cairculars for 'im.

[*He showers cards, commending somebody's self-adjusting trousers amongst the Audience, each person receiving about two dozen—chiefly in the eye—until the air is dark, and the floor thick with them.*

THE M. IN E. D. (*much annoyed*). Infernal liberty ! Confounded impudence ! Shouldn't have had *my* hat if I'd known he was going to play the fool with it like this !

FIRST LADY IN PLUSH CLOAK. But I thought you knew what was coming?

THE M. IN E. D. So I did—but this fellow does it differently.

[HERR VON K. *is preparing to fire a marked half-crown from a blunderbuss into a crystal casket.*

A LADY WITH NERVES (*to her husband*). John, I'm *sure* he's going to let that thing off!

JOHN (*a Brute*). Well, I shouldn't be surprised if he is. *I* can't help it.

THE L. WITH N. You could if you liked—you could tell him my nerves won't stand it—the trick will be every *bit* as good if he only *pretends* to fire, I'm sure.

JOHN. Oh, nonsense!—You can stand it very well if you *like*.

THE L. WITH N. I *can't*, John . . . . There, he's raising it to his shoulder. John, I *must* go out. I shall scream if I sit here, I *know* I shall!

JOHN. No, no—what's the use? He'll have fired long before you get to the door. Much better stay where you are, and do your screaming sitting down. (*The Conjuror fires.*) There, you see, you *didn't* scream, after all!

THE L. WITH N. I screamed to *myself*—which is ever so much worse for me; but you never *will* understand me till it's too late!

[HERR VON K. *performs another trick.*

FIRST LADY IN PLUSH CLOAK. That was very clever, wasn't it? I can't *imagine* how it was done!

THE M. IN E. D. (*in whom the memory of his desecrated hat is still rankling*). Oh, can't you? Simplest thing in the world—any child could do it!

SECOND LADY. What, find the rabbit inside those boxes, when they were all corded up, and sealed!

THE M. IN E. D. You don't mean to say you were taken in by *that!* Why, it was another rabbit, of course!

FIRST LADY. But even if it *was* another rabbit, it was wearing the borrowed watch round its neck.

THE M. IN E. D. Easy enough to slip the watch in, if all the boxes have false bottoms.

SECOND L. Yes, but he passed the boxes round for us to examine.

THE M. IN E. D. Boxes—but not *those* boxes.

FIRST L. But how could he slip the watch in when somebody was holding it all the time in a paper bag?

THE M. IN E. D. Ah, *I* saw how it was done—but it would take too long to explain it now. I *have* seen it so well performed that you *couldn't* spot it. But this chap's a regular duffer!

HERR V. K. (*who finds this sort of thing rather disturbing*). Lyties and Shentilmans, I see zere is von among us who is a brofessional like myself, and knows how all my leedle dricks is done. Now— [*suddenly abandoning his accent*]—I am always griteful for hanythink that will distrack the attention of the orjence from what is going on upon the Stige; naterally so, because it prevents you from follerin' my actions too closely, and so I now call upon this gentleman in the hevenin' dress jest to speak hup a very little louder than what he 'as been doin', so that you will be enabled to 'ear hevery word of 'is hexplanation more puffickly than what some of you in the back benches have done itherto. Now, Sir, if you'll kindly repeat your very hinteresting remarks in a more haudible tone, I can go on between like. [*Murmurs of " No no!" " Shut up!" " We don't want to hear him!" from various places;* THE MAN IN EVENING DRESS *subsides into a crimson taciturnity, which continues during the remainder of the performance.*

At the Tudor Exhibition.

IN THE CENTRAL HALL.

The usual Jocose 'ARRY (*who has come here with* 'ARRIET, *for no very obvious reason, as they neither of them know or care about any history but their own*). Well, I s'pose as we *are* 'ere, we'd better go in a buster for a book o' the words, eh? (*To* COMMISSIONAIRE.) What are yer doin' them c'rect guides at, ole man? A shillin'? Not *me!* 'Ere, 'Arriet, we'll make it out for ourselves.

A YOUNG MAN (*who has dropped in for five minutes—"just to say he's been, don't you know"*). 'Jove—my Aunt! Nip out before she spots me . . . Stop, though, suppose she *has* spotted me? Never can tell with giglamps . . . better not risk it.   [*Is " spotted" while hesitating.*

HIS AUNT. I didn't recognise you till just this moment, John, my boy. I was just wishing I had some one to read out all the extracts in the Catalogue for me ; now we can go round together.

> [JOHN *affects a dutiful delight at this suggestion, and wonders mentally if he can get away in time to go to afternoon tea with those pretty Chesterton Girls.*

AN UNCLE (*who has taken* MASTER TOMMY *out for the afternoon*). This is the way to make your English History *real* to you, my boy !

> [TOMMY, *who had cherished hopes of Covent Garden Circus, privately thinks that English History is a sufficiently unpleasant reality as it is, and conceives a bitter prejudice against the entire Tudor Period on the spot.*

THE INTELLIGENT PERSON. Ha! armour of the period, you see !

"WHAT ARE YOU DOIN' THEM C'RECT GUIDES AT, OLE MAN? A SHILLIN'? NOT *me!*"

(*Feels bound to make an intelligent remark.*) 'Stonishing how the whole art of war has been transformed since then, eh ? Now—to me—(*as if he was conscious of being singular in this respect*)—to *me*, all this is most interesting. Coming as I do, fresh from Froude—

His Companion (*a Flippant Person*). Don't speak so loud. If they know you've come in here fresh, you'll get turned out !

Patronising Persons (*inspecting magnificent suit of russet and gilt armour*). 'Pon my word, no idea they turned out such good work in those times—very creditable to them, really.

BEFORE THE PORTRAITS.

The Uncle. Now, Tommy, you remember what became of Katherine of Aragon, I'm sure ? No, no—tut—tut—*she* wasn't executed ! I'm afraid you're getting rather rusty with these long holidays. Remind me to speak to your mother about setting you a chapter or so of history to read every day when we get home, will you ?

Tommy (*to himself*). It *is* hard lines on a chap having a Sneak for an Uncle ! Catch me swotting to please *him !*

'Arry. There's old 'Enery the Eighth, you see—that's 'im right enough ; him as 'ad all those wives, and cut every one of their 'eds off !

'Arriet (*admiringly*). Ah, I knew we shouldn't want a Catalogue.

The Int. P. Wonderfully Holbein's caught the character of the man—the—er—curious compound of obstinacy, violence, good-humour, sensuality, and—and so on. No mistaking a Holbein—you can tell him at once by the extraordinary finish of all the accessories. Now look at that girdle—isn't that Holbein all over ?

Flippant P. Not quite all over, old fellow. Catalogue says it's painted by Paris Bordone.

The Int. P. Possibly—but it's Holbein's *manner*, and, looking at these portraits, you see at once how right Froude's estimate was of the King.

F. P. Does Froude say how he got that nasty one on the side of his nose ?

A Visitor. Looks overfed, don't he ?

SECOND V. (*sympathetically*). Oh, he fed himself very well; you can see that.

THE AUNT. Wait a bit, John—don't read so fast. I haven't made out the middle background yet. And where's the figure of St. Michael rising above the gilt tent, lined with *fleurs-de-lis* on a blue ground? Would this be Guisnes, or Ardres, now? Oh, Ardres on the right—so *that's* Ardres—yes, yes; and now tell me what it says about the two gold fountains, and that dragon up in the sky.

> [JOHN *calculates that, at this rate, he has a very poor chance of getting away before the Gallery closes.*

THE PATRONISING PERSONS. 'Um! Holbein again, you see—very curious their ideas of painting in those days. Ah, well, Art has made great progress since then—like everything else!

MISS FISHER. So *that's* the beautiful Queen Mary! I wonder if it is really *true* that people have got better-looking since those days?

> [*Glances appealingly at* PHLEGMATIC FIANCÉ.

HER PHLEGMATIC FIANCÉ. I wonder.

MISS F. You hardly ever see such small hands now, do you? With those lovely long fingers, too!

THE PHL. F. No, never.

MISS F. Perhaps people in some other century will wonder how anybody ever saw anything to admire in *us?*

THE PHL. F. Shouldn't be surprised.

> [MISS F. *does wish secretly that* CHARLES *had more conversation.*

THE AUNT. John, just find out who No. 222 is.

JOHN (*sulkily*). Sir George Penruddocke, Knight.

HIS AUNT (*with enthusiasm*). Of course—*how* interesting this is, isn't it?—seeing all these celebrated persons exactly as they were in life! Now read who he *was*, John, please.

THE INT. PERSON. Froude tells a curious incident about—

FLIPPANT P. I tell you what it is, old chap, if you read so much history, you'll end by *believing* it!

THE INT. P. (*pausing before the Shakspeare portraits*). "He was not for an age, but for all time."

THE FL. P. I suppose that's why they've painted none of them alike.

A PERSON WITH A TALENT FOR COMPARISON. Mary, come here a moment. Do look at this—"Elizabeth, Lady Hoby"—did you *ever* see such a likeness?

MARY. Well, dear, I don't quite—

THE PERSON WITH, &c. It's her living image! Do you mean to say you really don't recognise it?—Why, *Cook*, of course!

MARY. Ah! (*apologetically*)—but I've never seen her dressed to go *out*, you know.

THE UNCLE. "No. 13, Sir Rowland Hill, Lord Mayor, died 1561"—

TOMMY (*anxious to escape the threatened chapters if possible*). I know about *him*, Uncle, he invented postage stamps!

OVER THE CASES.

FIRST PATRONISING P. "A Tooth of Queen Katherine Parr." Dear me! very quaint.

SECOND P. P. (*tolerantly*). And not at all a bad tooth, either.

'ARRIET (*comes to a case containing a hat labelled as formerly belonging to Henry the Eighth*). 'Arry, look 'ere; fancy a king going about in a thing like that—pink with a green feather! Why, I wouldn't be seen in it myself!

'ARRY. Ah, but that was ole 'Enery all over, that was; *he* wasn't one for show. He liked a quiet, unassumin' style of 'at, he did. "None of yer loud pot 'ats for Me!" he'd tell the Royal 'atters; "find me a tile as won't attract people's notice, or you won't want a tile yerselves in another minute!" An' you may take yer oath they served him pretty *sharp*, too!

'ARRIET (*giggling*). It's a pity they didn't ask you to write their Catalogue for 'em.

THE AUNT. John, you're not really *looking* at that needlework—it's Queen Elizabeth's own work, John. Only look how wonderfully fine the stitches are. Ah, she was a truly *great* woman! I could spend hours over this case alone. What, closing are they, *already?* We must have another day at this together, John—just you and I.

JOHN. Yes, Aunt. And now—(*thinks there is just time to call on the* Chestertons, *if he goes soon*)—can I get you a cab, or put you into a 'bus or anything?

HIS AUNT. Not just yet; you must take me somewhere where I can get a bun and a cup of tea first, and then we can go over the Catalogue together, and mark all the things we *missed*, you know.

> [JOHN *resigns himself to the inevitable rather than offend his* *wealthy relative; the* INTELLIGENT PERSON *comes out,* *saying he has had "an intellectual treat," and intends to "run* *through Froude again" that evening.* 'ARRY *and* 'ARRIET, *depart to the "Ocean Wave" at Hengler's. Gallery gradually* *clears as Scene closes in.*

In an Omnibus.

The majority of the inside passengers, as usual, sit in solemn silence, and gaze past their opposite neighbours into vacancy. A couple of Matrons converse in wheezy whispers.

FIRST MATRON. Well, I must say a bus is pleasanter riding than what they used to be not many years back, and then so much cheaper, too. Why you can go all the way right from here to Mile End Road for threepence!

SECOND MATRON. What, all that way for threepence—(*with an impulse of vague humanity*). The *poor* 'orses!

FIRST MATRON. Ah, well, my dear, it's Competition, you know,—it don't do to think too much of it.

CONDUCTOR (*stopping the bus*). Orchard Street, Lady!

[*To* SECOND MATRON, *who had desired to be put down there.*

SECOND MATRON *to* CONDUCTOR). Just move on a few doors further, opposite the boot-shop. (*To* FIRST MATRON.) It will save us walking.

CONDUCTOR. Cert'inly, Mum, we'll drive in and wait while you're tryin' 'em on, if you like—*we* ain't in no 'urry!

[*The* MATRONS *get out, and their places are taken by two young girls, who are in the middle of a conversation of thrilling interest.*

FIRST GIRL. I never liked her myself—ever since the way she behaved at his Mother's that Sunday.

SECOND GIRL. How *did* she behave?

[*A faint curiosity is discernible amongst the other passengers to learn how she—whoever she is—behaved that Sunday.*

FIRST GIRL. Why, it was you *told* me! *You* remember. That night Joe let out about her and the automatic scent fountain.

SECOND GIRL. Oh, yes, I remember now. (*General disappointment.*) I couldn't help laughing myself. Joe didn't ought to have told—but she needn't have got into such a state over it, *need* she?

FIRST GIRL. That was Eliza all over. If George had been sensible, he'd have broken it off then and there—but no, he wouldn't hear a word against her, not at that time—it was the button-hook opened *his* eyes!

[*The other passengers strive to dissemble a frantic desire to know how and why this delicate operation was performed.*

SECOND GIRL (*mysteriously*). And enough too! But what put George off most was her keeping that bag so quiet.

[*The general imagination is once more stirred to its depths by this mysterious allusion.*

FIRST GIRL. Yes, he did feel that, I know, he used to come and go on about it to me by the hour together. "I shouldn't have minded so much," he told me over and over again, with the tears standing in his eyes,—"if it hadn't been that the bottles was all silver-mounted!"

SECOND GIRL. Silver-mounted? I never heard of *that* before—no wonder he felt hurt!

FIRST GIRL (*impressively*). Silver tops to every one of them—and that girl to turn round as she did, and her with an Uncle in the oil and colour line, too—it nearly broke George's 'art!

SECOND GIRL. He's such a one to take on about things—but, as I said to him, "George," I says, "You must remember it might have been worse. Suppose you'd been married to that girl, and *then* found out about Alf and the Jubilee sixpence—how would *that* have been?"

FIRST GIRL (*unconsciously acting as the mouthpiece of the other passengers*). And what did he say to *that?*

SECOND GIRL. Oh, nothing—there was nothing he *could* say, but I could see he was struck. She behaved very mean to the last—she wouldn't send back the German concertina.

FIRST GIRL. You don't say so! Well, I wouldn't have thought that of her, bad as she is.

SECOND GIRL. No, she stuck to it that it wasn't like a regular present, being got through a grocer, and as she couldn't send him back the tea, being drunk,—but did you hear how she treated Emma over the crinoline 'at she got for her?

FIRST GIRL (*to the immense relief of the rest*). No, what was that?

SECOND GIRL. Well, I had it from Emma her own self. Eliza wrote up to her and says, in a postscript like,—Why, this is Tottenham Court Road, I get out here. Good-bye, dear, I must tell you the rest another day.

> [*Gets out, leaving the tantalised audience inconsolable, and long-ing for courage to question her companion as to the precise details of Eliza's heartless behaviour to George. The companion, however, relapses into a stony reserve. Enter a* CHATTY OLD GENTLEMAN *who has no secrets from any-body, and of course selects as the first recipient of his confidence the one person who hates to be talked to in an omnibus.*

THE CHATTY O. G. I've just been having a talk with the policeman at the corner there—what do you think I said to him?

HIS OPPOSITE NEIGHBOUR. I—I really don't know.

THE C. O. G. Well, I told him he was a rich man compared to me. He said "I only get thirty shillings a week, Sir." "Ah," I said, "but look at your expenses, compared to mine. What would *you* do if you had to spend eight hundred a-year on your children's education?" I spend that—every penny of it, Sir.

HIS OPP. N. (*utterly uninterested*). Do you indeed?—dear me!

C. O. G. Not that I grudge it—a good education is a fortune in itself, and as I've always told my boys, they must make the best of it, for it's all they'll get. They're good enough lads, but I've had a deal of trouble with them one way and another—a *deal* of trouble. (*Pauses for some expression of sympathy—which does not come—and he continues:*) There are my two eldest sons—what must they do but fall in love with the same lady—the same lady, Sir! (*No one seems to care much for these domestic revelations—possibly because they are too obviously addressed to the general ear).* And, to make matters worse, she was a married woman—*(his principal hearer looks another way uneasily)*— the wife of a godson of mine, which made it all the more awkward, y'know. (HIS OPPOSITE NEIGHBOUR *giving no sign, the* C. O. G. *tries one Passenger after another.*) Well, I went to him—*(here he fixes an old Lady, who immediately passes up coppers out of her glove to the* CONDUCTOR) —I went to him, and said—*(addressing a smartly dressed young Lady with a parcel who giggles)*—I said, "You're a man of the world—so am I. Don't you take any notice," I told him—*(this to a callow young man, who blushes)*—"they're a couple of young fools," I said, "but you tell your dear wife from me not to mind those boys of mine—they'll soon get tired of it if they're only let alone." And so they would have, long ago, it's my belief, if they'd met with no encouragement—but what can *I* do—it's a heavy trial to a father, you know. Then there's my third son—he must needs go and marry—*(to a Lady at his side with a reticule, who gasps faintly)*—some young woman who dances at a Music-hall—nice daughter-in-law that for a man in my position, eh? I've forbidden him the house of course, and told his mother not to have any communication with him —but I know, Sir,—*(violently, to a Man on his other side, who coughs in much embarrassment)*—I *know* she meets him once a week under the eagle in Orme Square, and *I* can't stop her! Then I'm worried about my daughters—one of 'em gave me no peace till I let her have some painting lessons—of course, I naturally thought the drawing-master would be an elderly man—whereas, as things turned out,——

A QUIET MAN IN A CORNER. I 'ope you told all this to the Police-man, Sir?

THE C. O. G. *(flaming unexpectedly).* No, Sir, I did *not.* I am not in the habit—whatever *you* may be—of discussing my private affairs with strangers. I consider your remark highly impertinent, Sir.

[Fumes in silence for the rest of the journey.

THE YOUNG LADY WITH THE PARCEL *(to her friend—for the sake of vindicating her gentility).* Oh, my dear, I do feel so funny, carrying a great brown-paper parcel, in a bus, too! Any one would take me for a shop-girl!

"GO 'OME, DIRTY DICK!"

A GRIM OLD LADY OPPOSITE. And I only hope, my dear, you'll never be taken for any one less respectable.

[*Collapse of* GENTEEL Y.L.

FIRST HUMOROUS 'ARRY (*recognising a friend on entering*). Excuse me stoppin' your kerridge, old man, but I thought you wouldn't mind givin' me a lift, as you was goin' my way.

SECOND H. 'A. Quite welcome, old chap, so long as you give my man a bit when you git down, yer know.

FIRST H. 'A. Oh, o' course—that's expected between gentlemen. (*Both look round to see if their facetiousness is appreciated, find it is not and subside.*)

THE CONDUCTOR. Benk, benk! (*he means "Bank"*) 'Oborn, benk! 'Igher up there, Bill, can't you?

A DINGY MAN SMOKING, IN A VAN. Want to block up the ole o' the road, eh? That's right!

THE CONDUCTOR (*roused to personality*). Go 'ome, Dirty Dick! syme old soign, I see,—"Monkey an' Poipe!" (*To Coachman of smart brougham which is pressing rather closely behind.*) I say old man, don't you race after my bus like this—you'll only tire your 'orse.

[*The Coachman affects not to have heard.*

THE CONDUCTOR (*addressing the brougham horse, whose head is almost through the door of the omnibus*). 'Ere, 'ang it all!—step insoide, if yer want to!

[*Brougham falls to rear—triumph of* CONDUCTOR *as Scene closes.*

At a Sale of High=Class Sculpture.

SCENE—*An upper floor in a City Warehouse; a low whitewashed room, dimly lighted by dusty windows and two gas-burners in wire cages. Around the walls are ranged several statues of meek aspect, securely confined in barred wooden cases, like a sort of marble menagerie. In the centre, a labyrinthine grove of pedestals, surmounted by busts, groups, and statuettes by modern Italian masters. About these pedestals a small crowd—consisting of Elderly Merchants on the look out for a "neat thing in statuary" for the conservatory at Croydon or Muswell Hill, Young City Men who have dropped in after lunch, Disinterested Dealers, Upholsterers' Buyers, Obliging Brokers, and Grubby and Mysterious men—is cautiously circulating.*

OBLIGING BROKER (*to* AMIABLE SPECTATOR, *who has come in out of curiosity, and without the remotest intention of purchasing sculpture*). No Catlog, Sir? 'Ere, allow me to orfer you mine—that's *my* name in pencil on the top of it, Sir; and, if you *should* 'appen to see any lot that takes your fancy, you jest ketch my eye. (*Reassuringly.*) I sha'n't be fur off. Or look 'ere, gimme a nudge—I shall know what it means.

> [*The* A. S. *thanks him profusely, and edges away with an inward vow to avoid his and the* AUCTIONEER'S *eyes, as he would those of a basilisk.*

AUCTIONEER (*from desk, with the usual perfunctory fervour*). Lot 13, Gentlemen, very charming pair of subjects from child life—"*The Pricked Finger*" and "*The Scratched Toe*"—by Bimbi.

A STOLID ASSISTANT (*in shirtsleeves*). Figgers 'ere, Gen'lm'n!

> [*Languid surge of crowd towards them.*

"FIGGERS 'ere, GEN'L'M'N!"

A FACETIOUS BIDDER. Which of 'em's the finger and which the toe?

AUCT. (*coldly*). I should have thought it was easy to identify by the attitude. Now, Gentlemen, give me a bidding for these very finely-executed works by Bimbi. Make any offer. What will you give me for 'em? Both very sweet things, Gentlemen. Shall we say ten guineas?

A GRUBBY MAN. Give yer five.

AUCT. (*with grieved resignation*). Very well, start 'em at five. Any advance on five? (*To* ASSIST.) Turn 'em round, to show the back view. And a 'arf! Six! And a 'arf! Only six and a 'arf bid for this beautiful pair of figures, done direct from nature by Bimbi. Come, Gentlemen, come! Seven! Was that *you*, MR. GRIMES? (THE GRUBBY MAN *admits the soft impeachment.*) Seven and a 'arf. Eight! It's *against* you.

MR. GRIMES (*with a supreme effort*). Two-and-six!

[*Mops his brow with a red cotton handkerchief.*

AUCT. (*in a tone of gratitude for the smallest mercies*). Eight-ten-six. All done at eight-ten-six? Going . . . gone! GRIMES, Eight, ten, six. Take money for 'em. Now we come to a very 'andsome work by Piffalini—"*The Ocarina Player*," one of this great artist's masterpieces, and an exceedingly choice and high-class work, as you will all agree directly you see it. (*To* ASSIST.) Now, then, Lot 14, there—look sharp!

STOLID ASSIST. "Hocarina Plier" eyn't arrived, Sir.

AUCT. Oh, hasn't it? Very well, then. Lot 15. "*The Pretty Pill-taker*," by Antonio Bilio—a really magnificent work of Art, Gentlemen. ("*Pill-taker, 'ere!*" *from the* S. A.) What'll you give me for her? Come, make me an offer. (*Bidding proceeds till the "Pill-taker" is knocked down for twenty-three-and-a-half guineas.*) Lot 16, "*The Mixture as Before*," by same artist—make a charming and suitable companion to the last lot. What do you say, MR. MIDDLEMAN—take it at the same bidding? (Mr. M. *assents, with the end of one eyebrow.*) Any advance on twenty-three and a 'arf? None? Then,—MIDDLEMAN, Twenty-four, thirteen, six.

MR. MIDDLEMAN (*to the* AMIABLE SPECTATOR, *who has been vaguely inspecting the "Pill-taker"*). Don't know if you noticed it, Sir, but I got that last couple very cheap—on'y forty-seven guineas the pair, and they are worth eighty, I solemnly declare to you. I could get forty a piece for 'em to-morrow, upon my word and honour, I could. Ah, and I know who'd *give* it me for 'em, too!

THE A. S. (*sympathetically*). Dear me, then you've done very well over it.

MR. M. Ah, well ain't the word—and those two aren't the only lots I've got either. That "*Sandwich-Man*" over there is mine—look at the work in those boards, and the nature in his clay pipe ; and "*The Boot-Black*," that's mine, too—all worth twice what *I* got 'em for—and lovely things, too, ain't they?

THE A. S. Oh, very nice, very clever—congratulate you, I'm sure.

MR. M. I can see you've took a fancy to 'em, Sir, and, when I come across a gentleman that's a connysewer, I'm always sorry to stand in his light ; so, see here, you can have any one you like out o' my little lot, or all on 'em, with all the pleasure in the wide world, Sir, and I'll on'y charge you five per cent. on what I gave for 'em, and be exceedingly obliged to you, into the bargain, Sir. (*The A. S. feebly disclaims any desire to take advantage of this magnanimous offer.*) Don't say No, if you mean Yes, Sir. Will you 'ave "*The Pill-taker*," Sir ?

THE A. S. (*politely*). Thank you very much, but—er—I think *not.*

MR. M. Then perhaps you could do with "*The Little Boot-Black*," or "*The Sandwich-Man*," Sir ?

THE A. S. Perhaps—but I could do still better *without* them.

[*He moves to another part of the room.*

THE OBL. BROKER (*whispering beerily in his ear*). Seen anythink yet as takes your fancy, Sir ; 'cos, if so—

[*The* A. S. *escapes to a dark corner—where he is warmly welcomed by* MR. MIDDLEMAN.

MR. M. *Knew* you'd think better on it, Sir. Now which is it to be—the "*Boot-Black*," or "*Mixture as Before*" ?

AUCT. Now we come to Lot 19. Massive fluted column in coral marble with revolving-top—a column, Gentlemen, which will speak for itself.

THE FACETIOUS BIDDER (*after a scrutiny*). Then it may as well mention, while it's *about* it, that it's got a bit out of its back !

AUCT. Flaw in the marble, that's all. (*To* ASSIST.) Nothing the *matter* with the column, is there?

ASSIST. (*with reluctant candour*). Well, it 'as got a little chipped, Sir.

AUCT. (*easily*). Oh, very well then, we'll sell it "'A. F." Very glad it was found out in time, I'm sure. [*Bidding proceeds.*

FIRST DEALER *to* SECOND (*in a husky whisper*). Talkin' o' Old Masters, I put young 'Anway up to a good thing the other day.

SECOND D. (*without surprise—probably from a knowledge of his friend's noble unselfish nature*). Ah—'ow was that?

FIRST D. Well, there was a picter as I 'appened to know could be got in for a deal under what it ought—in good 'ands, mind yer—to fetch. It was a Morlan'—leastwise, it was so like you couldn't ha' told the difference, if you understand my meanin'. (*The other nods with complete intelligence.*) Well, I 'adn't no openin' for it myself just then, so I sez to young 'Anway, "You might do worse than go and 'ave a *look* at it," I told him. And I run against him yesterday, Wardour Street way, and I sez, "Did yer go and *see* that picter?" "Yes," sez he, "and what's more, I got it at pretty much my own figger, too!" "Well," sez I, "and ain't yer goin' to *shake 'ands with me over it?*"

SECOND D. (*interested*). And *did* he?

FIRST D. Yes, he did—he beyaved very fair over the matter, I will say *that* for him.

SECOND D. Oh, 'Anway's a very decent little feller—*now.*

AUCT. (*hopefully*). Now, Gentlemen, this next lot'll tempt you, *I'm* sure! Lot 33, a magnificent and very finely executed dramatic group out of the "*Merchant of Venice,*" *Othello* in the act of smothering *Desdemona,* both nearly life-size. (ASSIST., *with a sardonic inflection.* "*Group* 'ere, *Gen'lm'n!*") What shall we say for this great work by Roccocippi, Gentlemen? A hundred guineas, just to start us?

THE F. B. Can't you put the two figgers up separate?

AUCT. You know better than that—being a group, Sir. Come, come, any one give me a hundred for this magnificent marble group! The figure of *Othello* very finely finished, Gentlemen.

THE F. B. I should ha' thought it was *her* who was the finely finished one of the two.

AUCT. (*pained by this levity*). Really, Gentlemen, do 'ave more appreciation of a 'igh-class work like this! . . . Twenty-five guineas? . . . Nonsense! I can't put it up at that.

[*Bidding languishes. Lot withdrawn.*

SECOND DISINTERESTED DEALER (*to First D. D., in an undertone*). I wouldn't tell every one, but I shouldn't like to see *you* stay 'ere and waste your time; so, in case you *was* thinking of waiting for that last lot, I may just as well mention—

[*Whispers.*

FIRST D. D. Ah, it's *that* way, is it? Much obliged to you for the 'int. But I'd do the same for you any day.

SECOND D. D. I'm *sure* yer would!

[*They watch one another suspiciously.*

AUCT. Now 'ere's a tasteful thing, Gentlemen. Lot. 41. "*Nymph eating Oysters*" ("*Nymph 'ere, Gen'lm'n!*"), by the celebrated Italian artist Vabene, one of the finest works of Art in this room, and they're *all* exceedingly fine works of Art; but this is a *truly* work of Art, Gentlemen. What shall we say for her, eh? (*Silence.*) Why, Gentlemen, no more appreciation than *that?* Come, don't be afraid of it. Make a beginning. (*Bidding starts.*) Forty-five guineas. Forty-six—*pounds.* Forty-six pounds only, this remarkable specimen of modern Italian Art. Forty-six and a 'arf. Only forty-six ten bid for it. Give character to any gentleman's collection, a figure like this would. Forty-seven *pounds—guineas!* and a 'arf. . . . Forty-seven and a 'arf guineas . . . For the last time! Bidding with you, Sir. Forty-seven guineas and a 'arf—Gone! Name, Sir, if *you* please. Oh, money? Very well. Thank you.

PROUD PURCHASER (*to Friend, in excuse for his extravagance*). You see, I must have something for that grotto I've got in the grounds.

HIS FRIEND. If she was mine, I should put her in the hall, and have a gaslight fitted in the oyster-shell.

P. P. (*thoughtfully*). Not a bad idea. But electric light would be more suitable, and easier to fix too. Yes—we'll see.

THE OBL. BROKER (*pursuing the* AM. SPECT.).   I 'ope, Sir, you'll remember me, next time you're this way.

THE AM. SPECT. (*who has only ransomed himself by taking over an odd lot, consisting of imitation marble fruit, a model, under crystal, of the Leaning Tower of Pisa, and three busts of Italian celebrities of whom he has never heard*).   I'm afraid I sh'an't have very much chance of forgetting you.   *Good* afternoon !

[*Exit hurriedly, dropping the fruit, as Scene closes.*

At the Guelph Exhibition.

IN THE CENTRAL HALL.

A THRIFTY VISITOR (*on entering*). Catalogue? No. What's the use of a Catalogue? Miserable thing, the size of a tract, that tells you nothing you don't know!

HIS WIFE (*indicating a pile of Catalogues on table*). Aren't *these* big enough for you?

THE THR. V. Those? Why they're big enough for the *London Directory!* Think I'm going to drag a thing like that about the place? You don't really want a Catalogue—it's all your fancy!

MR. PRATTLER (*to* MISS AMMERSON). Oh, *do* stop and look at these *sweet* goldfish! Pets! Don't you *love* them? *Aren't* they tame?

MISS AMMERSON. Wouldn't do to have them *wild*—might jump out and *bite* people, you know!

MR. P. It's *too* horrid of you to make fun of my poor little enthusiasms! But really,—couldn't we get something and feed them?— *Do* let's!

MISS A. I dare say you could get ham-sandwiches in the Restaurant— or chocolates.

MR. P. How unkind you are to me! But I don't care. (*Wilfully.*) I shall come here all by myself, and bring biscuits. Great big ones! Are you determined to take me into that big room with all the Portraits? Well you must tell me who they all are, then, and which are the Guelphiest ones.

"PETS! DON'T YOU *love* THEM? *Aren't* THEY TAME?"

IN THE ROYAL ROOM.

CONSIDERATE NIECE (*to* UNCLE). They seem mostly Portraits here. You're sure you don't *mind* looking at them, Uncle? I know so many people *do* object to Portraits.

UNCLE (*with the air of a Christian Martyr*). No, my dear, no; *I* don't mind 'em. Stay here as long as you like. I'll sit down and look at the people till you've done.

FIRST CRITICAL VISITOR (*examining a View of St. James's Park*). I wonder where that was taken. In Scotland, I expect—there's two Highlanders there, you see.

SECOND C. V. Shouldn't wonder—lot o' work in that, all those different colours, and so many dresses. [*Admires, thoughtfully.*

A WELL-READ WOMAN. That's Queen Charlotte, that is. George the Third's wife, you know—her that was so *domestic*.

HER COMPANION. Wasn't that the one that was shut up in the Tower, or something?

THE W. W. In the Tower? Lor, my dear, no, *I* never 'eard of it. You're thinking of the Tudors, or some o' that lot, I expect!

HER COMP. Am I? I dare say. I never *could* remember 'Istry. Why, if you'll believe me, I always have to stop and think which of the Georges came first!

MORE CRITICAL VISITORS (*before Portraits*). He's rather pleasant-looking, don't you think? I *don't* like *her* face at all. So peculiar. And what a hideous dress—like a tea-gown without any upper part—frightful!

A SCEPTICAL V. They all seem to have had such thin lips in those days. Somehow, I *can't* bring myself to believe in such very thin lips—can *you*, dear?

HER FRIEND. I always think it's a sign of meanness, myself.

THE S. V. No; but I mean—I can't believe *every one* had them in the eighteenth century.

HER FRIEND. Oh, I don't know. If it was the fashion!

ABOUT THE CASES.

VISITOR (*admiring an embroidered waistcoat of the time of George the Second—a highly popular exhibit*). What lovely work! Why, it looks as if it was done yesterday!

HER COMPANION (*who is not in the habit of allowing his enthusiasm to run away with him*). Um—yes, it's not bad. But, of course, they wouldn't send a thing like that here without having it washed and done up first!

AN OLD LADY. "Teapot used by the Duke of Wellington during his campaigns." So he drank *tea*, did he? Dear me! Do you know, my dear, I think I must have *my* old tea-pot engraved. It will make it so much more interesting some day!

IN THE SOUTH GALLERY.

MR. PRATTLER (*before a portrait of Lady Hamilton by Romney*). There! Isn't she too charming? I do call her a perfect *duck!*

MISS AMMERSON. Yes, you mustn't forget her when you bring those biscuits.

AN AMURKCAN GIRL. Father, see up there; there's Byron. Did you erver see such a purrfectly beautiful face?

HER FATHER (*solemnly*). He was a beautiful *Man*—a beautiful Poet.

THE A. G. I know—but the *expression*, it's real saint-like!

FATHER (*slowly*). Well, I guess if he'd had any different kind of expression, he wouldn't have written the things he *did* write, and that's a fact!

A MORALISING OLD LADY (*at Case O*). No. 1260. "Ball of Worsted wound by William Cowper, the poet, for Mrs. Unwin." No. 1261. "Netting done by William Cowper, the poet." How very nice, and what a difference in the habit of literary persons *nowadays*, my dear!

IN THE CENTRAL HALL.

MR. WHITEROSE, *a Jacobite fin de siècle, is seated on a Bench beside a* SEEDY STRANGER.

THE S. S. (*half to himself*). Har, well, there's one comfort, these 'ere Guelphs'll get notice to quit afore we're *much* older!

MR. WHITEROSE (*surprised*). You say so? Then you too are of the Young England Party! I am rejoiced to hear it. You cheer me; it is a sign that the good Cause is advancing.

THE S. S. Advancin'? I believe yer. Why, I know a dozen and more as are workin' 'art and soul for it!

MR. W. You do? We are making strides, indeed! Our England has suffered these usurpers too long.

THE S. S. Yer right. But we'll chuck 'em out afore long, and it'll be " Over goes the Show " with the lot, eh?

MR. W. I had no idea that the—er—intelligent artisan classes were so heartily with us. We must talk more of this. Come and see me. Bring your friends—all you can depend upon. Here is my card.

THE S. S. (*putting the card in the lining of his hat*). Right, Guv'nor; we'll come. I wish there was more gents like yer, I do!

MR. W. We are united by a common bond. We both detest—do we not?—the Hanoverian interlopers. We are both pledged never to rest until we have brought back to the throne of our beloved England, her lawful sovereign lady—(*uncovering*)—our gracious Mary of Austria-Este, the legitimate descendant of Charles the Blessed Martyr!

THE S. S. 'Old on, Guv'nor! Me and my friends are with yer so fur as doing away with these 'ere hidle Guelphs; but blow yer Mary of Orstria, yer know. Blow 'er!

MR. W. (*horrified*). Hush—this is rank treason! Remember—she is the lineal descendant of the House of Stuart!

THE S. S. What of it? There won't be no lineal descendants when we git *hour* way, 'cause there won't be nothing to descend to nobody. The honly suv'rin *we* mean to 'ave is the People—the Democrisy.

But there, you're young, me and my friends'll soon tork you over to hour way o' thinking. I dessay we 'aint fur apart, as it is. I got yer address, and we'll drop in on yer some night—never fear. No hevenin' dress, o' course?

MR. W. Of course. I—I'll look out for you. But I'm seldom in —hardly *ever*, in fact.

THE S. S. Don't you fret about *that*. Me and my friends ain't nothing partickler to do just now. We'll *wait* for yer. I should like yer to know ole Bill Gabb. You should 'ear *that* feller goin' on agin the Guelphs when he's 'ad a little booze—it 'ud do your 'art good. Well, I on'y come in 'ere as a deligate like, to report, and I seen enough. So 'ere's good-day to yer.

MR W. (*alone*). I shall have to change my rooms—and I *was* so comfortable! Well, well,—another sacrifice to the Cause!

At the Royal Academy.

IN THE VESTIBULE.

Visitors ascending staircase, full of enthusiasm and energetic determination not to miss a single Picture, encounter people descending in various stages of mental and physical exhaustion. At the turnstiles two Friends meet unexpectedly; both being shy men, who, with timely notice, would have preferred to avoid one another, their greetings are marked by an unnatural effusion and followed by embarrassed silence.

FIRST SHY MAN (*to break the spell*). Odd, our running up against one another like this, eh?

SECOND SHY MAN. Oh, very odd. (*Looks about him irresolutely, and wonders if it would be decent to pass on. Decides it will hardly do.*) Great place for meeting, the Academy, though.

FIRST S. M. Yes; sure to come across *somebody*, sooner or later.

[*Laughs nervously, and wishes the other would go.*

SECOND S. M. (*seeing that his friend lingers*). This your *first* visit here?

FIRST S. M. Yes. Couldn't very well get away *before*, you know.

[*Feels apologetic, without exactly knowing why.*

SECOND S. M. It's *my* first visit, too. (*Sees no escape, and resigns himself.*) Er—we may as well go round together, eh?

FIRST S. M. (*who was afraid this was coming—heartily*). Good! By the way, I always think, on a first visit, it's best to take a single room, and do that thoroughly. [*This has only just occurred to him.*

SECOND S. M. (*who had been intending to follow that plan himself*). Oh, *do* you? Now, for *my* part, I don't attempt to see anything *thoroughly* the first time. Just scamper through, glance at the things one oughtn't to miss, get a general impression, and come away. *Then*, if I don't happen to come again, I've always *done* it, you see. But (*considerately*), look here. Don't let me drag you about, if you'd rather not!

FIRST S. M. Oh, but I shouldn't like to feel I was any tie on you. Don't you mind about me. I shall potter about in here—for hours, I dare say.

SECOND S. M. Ah, well (*with vague consolation*), I shall always know where to *find* you, I suppose.

FIRST S. M. (*brightening visibly*). Oh dear, yes; I sha'n't be far away.

> [*They part with mutual relief, only tempered by the necessity of following the course they have respectively prescribed for themselves. Nemesis overtakes the* SECOND S. M. *in the next Gallery, when he is captured by a Desultory Enthusiast, who insists upon dragging him all over the place to see obscure "bits" and "gems," which are only to be appreciated by ricking the neck or stooping painfully.*

A SUBURBAN LADY (*to Female Friend*). Oh dear, *how* stupid of me! I *quite* forgot to bring a pencil! Oh, *thank* you, dear, that will do *beautifully.* It's just a *little* blunt; but so long as I can *mark* with it, you know. You don't think we should avoid the crush if we began at the end room? Well, perhaps it *is* less confusing to begin at the beginning, and work steadily through.

IN GALLERY NO. I.

A small group has collected before Mr. Wyllie's "Davy Jones's Locker," which they inspect solemnly for some time before venturing to commit themselves to any opinion.

FIRST VISITOR (*after devoting his whole mind to the subject*). Why, it's the Bottom of the Sea—at least (*more cautiously*), that's what it seems to be *intended* for.

SECOND V. Ah, and very well done, too. I wonder, now, how he managed to stay down long enough to paint all that?

"CAPTURED BY A DESULTORY ENTHUSIAST."

THIRD V. Practice, I suppose. I've seen writing done under water myself. But that was a tank!

FOURTH V. (*presumably in profound allusion to the fishes and sea-anemones*). Well, they seem to be 'aving it all their own way down there, don't they?

[*The Group, feeling that this remark sums up the situation, disperses.*

THE SUBURBAN LADY (*her pencil in full play*). No. 93. Now what's *that* about? Oh, "*Forbidden Sweets*,"—yes, to be sure. *Isn't* that charming? Those two dear little tots having their tea, and the kitten with its head stuck in the jam-pot, and the label and all, and the sticky spoon on the nursery table-cloth—so *natural!* I really *must* mark that. (*Awards this distinction.*) 97. "*Going up Top.*" Yes, *of course.* Look, Lucy dear, that little fellow has just answered a question, and his master tells him he may go to the top of the class, do you *see?* And the big boy looking so sulky, he's wishing he had learnt his lesson better. I do think it's *so* clever—all the different expressions. Yes, I shall *certainly* mark that!

IN GALLERY NO. II.

THE S. L. (*doubtfully*). H'm, No. 156. "*Cloud Chariots*"? Not very *like* chariots, though, *are* they?

HER FRIEND. I expect it's one of those sort of pictures that you have to look at a long time, and then things gradually come *out* of it, you know.

THE S. L. It *may* be. (*Tries the experiment.*) No, *I* can't make *anything* come out—only just clouds and their reflections. (*Struggling between good-nature and conscientiousness.*) I *don't* think I *can* mark that.

IN GALLERY NO. III.

A MATRON (*before Mr. Dicksee's "Tannhäuser"*). "*Venus and Tannhäuser*"—ah, and is that Venus on the stretcher? Oh, *that's* her all on fire in the background. Then which is Tannhäuser, and what are they all supposed to be doing? [*In a tone of irritation.*

HER NEPHEW. Oh, it tells you all about it in the Catalogue—he meets her funeral, you know, and leaves grow on his stick.

THE MATRON (*pursing her lips*). Oh, a *dead person.*

[*Repulses the Catalogue severely and passes on.*

FIRST PERSON, *with an "Eye for Art"* (*before " Psyche's Bath," by the President*). Not bad, eh?

SECOND PERSON, &c. No, I rather like it. (*Feels that he is growing too lenient*). He doesn't give you a very good idea of marble, though.

FIRST P. &c. No—*that's* not marble, and he always puts too many folds in his drapery to suit *me*.

FIRST P. &c. Just what *I* always say. It's not natural, you know.

[*They pass on, much pleased with themselves and one another.*

A FIANCÉ (*halting before a sea-scape, by Mr. Henry Moore, to* FIANCÉE). Here, I say, hold on a bit—what's *this* one?

FIANCÉE (*who doesn't mean to waste the whole afternoon over pictures*). Why, it's only a lot of waves—*come* on!

THE SUBURBAN L. Lucy, *this* is rather nice. *" Breakfasts for the Porth !"* (*Pondering*). I think there must be a mistake in the Catalogue—I don't see any breakfast things—they're cleaning fish, and what's a " Porth!" Would you mark that—or not?

HER COMP. Oh, I *think* so.

THE S. L. I don't know. I've marked such a quantity already and the lead won't hold out much longer. Oh, it's by Hook, R.A. Then I suppose it's *sure* to be all right. I've marked it, dear.

DUET BY TWO DREADFULLY SEVERE YOUNG LADIES, *who paint a little on China.* Oh, my *dear*, look at that. Did you ever *see* such a thing? Isn't it too perfectly *awful?* And there's a thing! Do come and look at this horror over here. A *" Study,"* indeed. I should just think it *was!* Oh, Maggie, don't be so satirical, or I shall die! No, but *do* just see this—isn't it *killing?* They get worse and worse every year, I declare!

[*And so on.*

IN GALLERY NO. V.

Two Prosaic Persons come upon a little picture, by Mr. Swar, of a boy lying on a rock, piping to fishes.

FIRST P. P. *That's* a rum thing!

SECOND P. P. Yes, I wasn't aware myself that fishes were so partial to music.

FIRST P. P. They may be—out there—(*perceiving that the boy is unclad*)—but it's peculiar altogether—they look like herrings to me.

SECOND P. P. Yes—or mackerel. But (*tolerantly*) I suppose it's a fancy subject.

> [*They consider that this absolves them from taking any further interest in it, and pass on.*

IN GALLERY NO. XI.

AN OLD LADY (*who judges Art from a purely Moral Standpoint, halts approvingly before a picture of a female orphan*). Now that really *is* a nice picture, my dear—a plain black dress and white cuffs—just what I *like* to see in a young person !

THE S. L. (*her enthusiasm greatly on the wane, and her temper slightly affected*). Lucy, I *wish* you wouldn't worry so—it's quite impossible to stop and look at *everything*. If you wanted your tea as badly as *I* do ! Mark that one ? What, when they neither of them have a single *thing* on ! Never, Lucy,—and I'm surprised at your suggesting it ! Oh, you meant the next one ? h'm—no, I *can't* say I care for it. Well, if I *do* mark it, I shall only put a tick—for it really is *not* worth a cross !

COMING OUT.

THE MAN WHO ALWAYS MAKES THE RIGHT REMARK. H'm. Haven't seen anything I could carry away with me.

HIS FLIPPANT FRIEND. Too many people about, eh ? Never mind, old chap, you *may* manage to sneak an umbrella down stairs—I won't say anything !

> [*Disgust of his companion, who descends stairs in offended silence, as scene closes.*

At the Iborse Show.

TIME—*About* 3.30. *Leaping Competition about to begin. The Competitors are ranged in a line at the upper end of the Hall while the attendants place the hedges in position. Amongst the Spectators in the Area are— a Saturnine Stableman from the country ; a Cockney Groom ; a Morbid Man ; a Man who is apparently under the impression that he is the only person gifted with sight ; a Critic who is extremely severe upon other people's seats ; a Judge of Horseflesh ; and Two Women who can't see as well as they could wish.*

THE DESCRIPTIVE MAN. They've got both' the fences up now, d'ye see ? There's the judges. going to start the jumping; each rider's got a ticket with his number on his back. See ? The first man's horse don't seem to care about jumping this afternoon—see how he's dancing about. Now he's going at it—there, he's cleared it ! Now he'll have to jump the next one !

> [*Keeps up a running fire of these instructive and valuable observations throughout the proceedings.*

THE JUDGE OF HORSEFLESH. Rare good shoulders that one has.

THE SEVERE CRITIC (*taking the remark to apply to the horse's rider*). H'm, yes—rather—pity he sticks his elbows out quite so much, though.

> [*His Friend regards him in silent astonishment.*
> *Another Competitor clears a fence, but exhibits a considerable amount of daylight.*

THE SATURNINE STABLEMAN (*encouragingly*). You'll 'ev to set back a bit next journey, Guv'nor !

THE COCKNEY GROOM. 'Orses 'ud jump better if the fences was a bit 'igher.

THE S. S. They'll be plenty 'oigh enough fur some on 'em.

THE SEVERE CRITIC. Ugly seat that fellow has—all anyhow when the horse jumps.

JUDGE OF HORSEFLESH. Has he? I didn't notice—I was looking at the horse. [SEVERE CRITIC *feels snubbed.*

THE S. S. (*soothingly, as the Competitor with the loose seat comes round again*). *That's* not good, Guv'nor!

THE COCKNEY GROOM. 'Ere's a little bit o' fashion coming down next—why, there's quite a boy on his back.

THE S. S. 'E won't be on 'im long if he don't look out. Cup an ball *I* call it!

THE MORBID MAN. I suppose there's always a accident o' some sort before they've finished.

FIRST WOMAN. Oh, don't, for goodness' sake, talk like that—I'm sure *I* don't want to see nothing 'appen.

SECOND WOMAN. Well, you may make your mind easy—for you won't see nothing here; you *would* have it this was the best place to come to!

FIRST WOMAN. I only said there was no sense in paying extra for the balcony, when you can go in the area for nothing.

SECOND WOMAN (*snorting*). Area, indeed! It might be a good deal airier than what it is, I'm sure—I shall melt if I stay here much longer.

THE MORBID MAN, There's one thing about being so close to the jump as this—if the 'orse jumps sideways—as 'osses will do every now and then—he'll be right in among us before we know where we are, and then there'll be a pretty how-de-do!

SECOND WOMAN (*to her Friend*). Oh, come away, do—it's bad enough to see nothing, let alone having a great 'orse coming down atop of us, and me coming out in my best bonnet, too—come away! [*They leave.*

THE DESCRIPTIVE MAN. Now, they're going to make 'em do some in-and-out jumping, see? they're putting the fences close together—that'll puzzle some of them—ah, he's over both of 'em ; very clean that one jumps ! Over again ! He's got to do it all twice, you see.

THE JUDGE OF HORSEFLESH. Temperate horse, that chestnut.

THE SEVERE CRITIC. Is he, though ?—but I suppose they *have* to be here, eh ? Not allowed champagne or whiskey or anything before they go in—like they are on a race-course ?

THE J. OF H. No, they insist on every horse taking the pledge before they'll enter him.

THE DESCRIPTIVE MAN. Each of 'em's had a turn at the in-and-out jump now. What's coming next ? Oh, the five-barred gate—they're going over that now, and the stone wall—see them putting the bricks on top ? That's to *raise* it.

THE MORBID MAN. None of 'em been off yet ; but (*hopefully*) there'll be a nasty fall or two over this business—there's been many a neck broke over a lower gate than that.

[*A Competitor clears the gate easily, holding the reins casually in his right hand.*

THE J. OF H. That man can ride.

THE SEVERE CRITIC. Pretty well—not what I call *business*, though—going over a gate with one hand, like that.

THE J. OF H. Didn't know you were such an authority.

THE S. C. (*modestly*). Oh, I can tell when a fellow has a good seat. I used to ride a good deal at one time. Don't get the chance much now—worse luck !

THE J. OF H. Well, I can give you a chance, as it happens. (SEVERE CRITIC *accepts with enthusiasm, and the inward reflection that the chance is much less likely to come off than he is himself.*) You wait till the show is over, and they let the horses in for exercise. I know a man who's got a cob here—regular little devil to go—bucks a bit at times—but you won't mind that. I'll take you round to the stall and get my friend to let you try him on the tan. How will that do you, eh ?

THE SEVERE CRITIC (*almost speechless with gratitude*). Oh—er—it will *do* me right enough—capital! That is—it *would*, if I hadn't an appointment, and had my riding things on, and wasn't feeling rather out of sorts, and hadn't promised to go home and take my wife in the Park, and it's her birthday, too, and, then, I've long made it a rule never to mount a strange horse, and—er—so you understand how it is don't you?

THE J. OF H. Quite, my dear fellow. (*As, for that matter, he has done from the first.*)

THE COCKNEY GROOM (*alluding to a man who is riding at the gate*). 'Ere's a rough 'un this bloke's on! (*Horse rises at gate; his rider shouts "Hoo, over!" and the gate falls amidst general derision.*) Over? Ah, I should just think it *was* over !

THE SATURNINE STABLEMAN (*as horseman passes*). Yer needn't ha' "Hoo'd" for that much !

> [*The Small Boy, precariously perched on an immense animal, follows; his horse, becoming unmanageable, declines the gate, and leaps the hurdle at the side.*

THE S. S. Ah, you're a *artful* lad, you are—thought you'd take it where it was easiest, eh?—you'll 'ev to goo back and try agen you will.

CHORUS OF SYMPATHETIC BYSTANDERS. Take him at it again, boy; *you're* all right ! . . Hold him in tighter, my lad. . . . Let out your reins a bit ! Lor, they didn't ought to let a boy like that ride. . . . He ain't no more 'old on that big 'orse than if he was a fly on him ! . . . Keep his 'ed straighter next time. . . . Enough to try a boy's nerve ! &c., &c.

> [*The Boy takes the horse back, and eventually clears the gate amidst immense and well-deserved applause.*

THE MORBID MAN (*disappointed*). Well, I fully expected to see '*im* took off on a shutter.

THE DESCRIPTIVE MAN. It's the water-jump next—see; that's it in the middle; there's the water, underneath the hedge; they'll have to clear the 'ole of that—or else fall in and get a wetting. They've taken all the

"HE EXPECTED THERE WOULD HAVE BEEN MORE TO SEE."

horses round to the other entrance—they'll come in from that side directly.

> [*One of the Judges holds up his stick as a signal; wild shouts of "Hoy-hoy! Whorr-oosh!" from within, as a Competitor dashes out and clears hedge and ditch by a foot or two. Deafening applause. A second horseman rides at it, and lands —if the word is allowable—neatly in the water. Roars of laughter as he scrambles out.*

THE MORBID MAN. Call that a brook! It ain't a couple of inches deep—it's more mud than water! No fear (*he means "no hope"*) of any on 'em getting a ducking over that!

> [*And so it turns out; the horses take the jump with more or less success, but without a single saddle being vacated. The proceedings terminate for the afternoon amidst demonstrations of hearty satisfaction from all but* THE MORBID MAN, *who had expected there would have been "more to see."*

At a Dance.

THE HOSTESS *is receiving her Guests at the head of the staircase; a* CONSCIENTIOUSLY LITERAL MAN *presents himself.*

HOSTESS (*with a gracious smile, and her eyes directed to the people immediately behind him*). *So* glad you were able to come—how do you *do?*

THE CONSCIENTIOUSLY LITERAL MAN. Well, if you had asked me that question this afternoon, I should have said I was in for a severe attack of malarial fever—I had all the symptoms—but, about seven o'clock this evening, they suddenly passed off, and—

[*Perceives, to his surprise, that his Hostess's attention is wandering, and decides to tell her the rest later in the evening.*

MR. CLUMPSOLE. How do you do, Miss Thistledown? Can you give me a dance?

MISS THISTLEDOWN (*who has danced with him before*—once). With pleasure—let me see, the third extra after supper? Don't forget.

MISS BRUSKLEIGH (*to Major Erser*). Afraid I can't give you anything just now—but if you see me standing about later on, you can come and ask me again, you know.

MR. BOLDOVER (*glancing eagerly round the room as he enters, and soliloquising mentally*). She ought to be here by this time, if she's coming —can't see her though—she's certainly not dancing. There's her sister over there with the mother. She *hasn't* come, or she'd be with them. Poor-looking lot of girls here to-night—don't think much of this music— get away as soon as I can, no *go* about the thing! . . . Hooray! There she is, after all! Jolly waltz this is they're playing! How pretty she's looking—how pretty *all* the girls are looking! If I can only get her to give me one dance, and sit out most of it somewhere! I feel as if I could talk to her to-night. By Jove, I'll try it!

> [*Watches his opportunity, and is cautiously making his way towards his divinity, when he is intercepted.*

MRS. GRAPPLETON. Mr. Boldover, I do believe you were going to *cut* me! (*Mr. B. protests and apologises.*) Well, *I* forgive you. I've been wanting to have another talk with you for ever so long. I've been thinking so *much* of what you said that evening about Browning's relation to Science and the Supernatural. Suppose you take me down stairs for an ice or something, and we can have it out comfortably together.

> [*Dismay of* Mr. B., *who has entirely forgotten any theories he may have advanced on the subject, but has no option but to comply; as he leaves the room with* MRS. GRAPPLETON *on his arm, he has a torturing glimpse of* MISS ROUNDARM, *apparently absorbed in her partner's conversation.*

MR. SENIOR ROPPE (*as he waltzes*). Oh, you needn't feel convicted of extraordinary ignorance, I assure you, Miss Featherhead. You would be surprised if you knew how many really clever persons have found that simple little problem of nought divided by one too much for them. Would you have supposed, by the way, that there is a reservoir in Pennsylvania containing a sufficient number of gallons to supply all London for eighteen months? You don't quite realize it, I see. "How many gallons is that?" Well, let me calculate roughly—taking the population of London at four millions, and the average daily consumption for each individual at—no, I can't work it out with sufficient accuracy while I am dancing; suppose we sit down, and I'll do it for you on my shirt-cuff—oh, very well; then I'll work it out when I get home, and send you the result to-morrow, if you will allow me.

MR. CULDERSACK (*who has provided himself beforehand with a set of topics for conversation—to his partner, as they halt for a moment*). Er—(*consults some hieroglyphics on his cuff stealthily*)—have you read Stanley's book yet?

MISS TABULA RAISER. No, I haven't. Is it interesting?

MR. CULDERSACK. I can't say. I've not seen it myself. Shall we —er—? [*They take another turn.*

" ER—" (CONSULTS SOME HIEROGLYPHICS ON HIS CUFF STEALTHILY).

MR. C. I suppose you have—er—been to the (*hesitates between the Academy and the Military Exhibition—decides on latter topic as fresher*) Military Exhibition?

MISS T. R. No—not yet. What do you think of it?

MR. C. Oh—*I* haven't been either. Er—do you care to—?

[*They take another turn.*

MR. C. (*after third halt*). Er—do you take any interest in politics?

MISS T. R. Not a bit.

MR. C. (*much relieved*). No more do I. (*Considers that he has satisfied all mental requirements.*) Er—let me take you down stairs for an ice.

[*They go.*

MRS. GRAPPLETON (*re-entering with* MR. BOLDOVER, *after a discussion that has outlasted two ices and a plate of strawberries*). Well, I thought you would have explained my difficulties better than *that*—oh, what a *delicious* waltz! Doesn't it set you longing to dance?

MR. B. (*who sees* MISS ROUNDARM *in the distance, disengaged*). Yes, I really think I must— [*Preparing to escape.*

MRS. GRAPPLETON. I'm getting such an old thing, that really I oughtn't to—but well, just this *once*, as my husband isn't here.

[MR. BOLDOVER *resigns himself to necessity once more.*

FIRST CHAPERON (*to second ditto*). How sweet it is of your eldest girl to dance with that absurd Mr. Clumpsole! It's really too *bad* of him to make such an exhibition of her—one can't help smiling at them!

SECOND CH. Oh, Ethel never can bear to hurt any one's feelings—so different from some girls! By the way, I've not seen *your* daughter dancing to-night—men who dance are so scarce nowadays—I suppose they think they have the right to be a little fastidious.

FIRST CH. Bella has been out so much this week, that she doesn't care to dance except with a really first-rate partner. She is not so easily pleased as your Ethel, I'm afraid.

SECOND CH. Ethel is *young*, you see, and, when one is pressed so much to dance, one can hardly refuse, *can* one? When she has had as many seasons as BELLA, she will be less energetic, I dare say.

[MR. BOLDOVER *has at last succeeded in approaching* MISS ROUNDARM, *and even in inducing her to sit out a dance with him; but, having led her to a convenient alcove, he finds himself totally unable to give any adequate expression to the rapture he feels at being by her side.*

MR. B. (*determined to lead up to it somehow*). I—I was rather thinking —(*he* meant *to say, "devoutly hoping," but, to his own bitter disgust, it comes out like this*)—I should meet you here to-night.

MISS R. Were you? Why?

MR. B. (*with a sudden dread of going too far just yet*). Oh (*carelessly*), you know how one *does* wonder who will be at a place, and who won't.

MISS R. No, indeed, I don't—*how* does one wonder?

MR. B. (*with a vague notion of implying a complimentary exception in her case*). Oh, well, generally—(*with the fatal tendency of a shy man to a sweeping statement*)—one may be pretty sure of meeting just the people one least wants to see, you know.

MISS R. And so you thought you would probably meet me. I *see*.

MR. B. (*overwhelmed with confusion, and not in the least knowing what he says*). No, no, I didn't think that—I hoped you mightn't—I mean, I was afraid you might—

[*Stops short, oppressed by the impossibility of explaining.*

MISS R. You are not very complimentary to-night, are you?

MR. B. I can't pay compliments—to *you*—I don't know how it is, but I never can talk to you as I can to other people!

MISS R. Are you amusing when you are with other people?

MR. B. At all events I can find things to say to *them*.

Enter ANOTHER MAN.

ANOTHER MAN (*to* MISS R.). Our dance, I think?

MISS R. (*who had intended to get out of it*). I was wondering if you ever meant to come for it. (*To* MR. B., *as they rise.*) Now I sha'n't feel I am depriving the other people! (*Perceives the speechless agony in his expression, and relents.*) Well, you can have the next after this if you care about it—only *do* try to think of something in the meantime! (*As she goes off.*) You will—won't you?

MR. B. (*to himself*). She's given me another chance! If only I can rise to it. Let me see—what shall I begin with? *I* know—*Supper!* She hasn't been down yet.

HIS HOSTESS. Oh, Mr. Boldover, you're not dancing this—do be good and take some one down to supper—those poor Chaperons are dying for some food.

> [Mr. B. *takes down a Matron whose repast is protracted through three waltzes and a set of Lancers—he comes up to find* MISS ROUNDARM *gone, and the Musicians putting up their instruments.*

COACHMAN AT DOOR (*to Linkman, as* MR. B. *goes down the steps*). That's the *lot*, Jim!

> [Mr. B. *walks home, wishing the Park Gates were not shut, so as to render the Serpentine inaccessible.*

At the British Museum.

IN THE SCULPTURE GALLERIES.

Sightseers discovered drifting languidly along in a state of depression, only tempered by the occasional exercise of the right of every free-born Briton to criticize whenever he fails to understand. The general tone is that of faintly amused and patronizing superiority.

A BURLY SIGHTSEER *with a red face* (*inspecting group representing* "*Mithras Sacrificing a Bull*"). H'm; that may be Mithras's notion of making a clean job of it, but it ain't *mine !*

A WOMAN (*examining a fragment from base of sculptured column with a puzzled expression as she reads the inscription*). "Lower portion of female figure—probably a Bacchante." Well, how they know who it's intended for, when there ain't more than a bit of her skirt left, beats *me !*

HER COMPANION. Oh, I s'pose they've got to put a name to it o' *some* sort.

AN INTELLIGENT ARTISAN (*out for the day with his* FIANCÉE.—*reading from pedestal*). "Part of a group of As--Astrala—no, As*traga*—lizontes" —that's what *they* are, yer see.

FIANCÉE. But who *were* they ?

THE I. A. Well, I can't tell yer—not for certain ; but I expect they'd be the people who in'abited Astragalizontia.

FIANCÉE. Was that what they used to call Ostralia before it was discovered ? (*They come to the Clytie bust.*) Why, if that isn't the same

"H'M; THAT MAY BE MITHRAS'S NOTION OF MAKING A CLEAN JOB OF IT,
BUT IT AIN'T *mine!*"

head Mrs. Meggles has under a glass shade in her front window, only smaller—and hers is alabaster, too! But fancy them going and copying it, and I dare say without so much as a "by your leave," or a "thank you!"

THE I. A. (*reading*). "Portrait of Antonia, sister-in-law of the Emperor Tiberius, in the character of Clytie turning into a sunflower."

FIANCÉE. Lor! They did queer things in those days, didn't they? (*Stopping before another bust.*) Who's that?

THE I. A. 'Ed of Ariadne.

FIANCÉE (*slightly surprised*). What!—not young Adney down our street? I didn't know as he'd been took in stone.

THE I. A. How do you suppose they'd 'ave young Adney in among this lot—why, that's antique!

FIANCÉE. Well, I was *thinking* it looked more like a female. But if it's meant for old Mr. Teak the shipbuilder's daughter, it flatters her up considerable; and, besides, I always understood as her name was Betsy.

THE I. A. No, no; what a girl you are for getting things wrong! that 'ed was cut out years and years ago!

FIANCÉE. Well, she's gone off *since*, that's all; but I wonder at old Mr. Teak letting it go out of the family, instead of putting it on his mantelpiece along with the lustres, and the two chiny dogs.

THE A. I. (*with ungallant candour*). 'Ark at you! Why you 'ain't much more sense nor a chiny dog yourself!

MORALIZING MATRON (*before the Venus of Ostia*). And to think of the poor ignorant Greeks worshipping a shameless hussey like that! It's a pity they hadn't some one to teach them more respectable notions! Well, well! it ought to make us thankful *we* don't live in those benighted times, that it ought!

A CONNOISSEUR (*after staring at a colossal Greek lion*). A lion, eh? Well, it's another proof to my mind that the ancients hadn't got very far in the statuary line. Now, if you *want* to see a stone lion done true to Nature, you've only to walk any day along the Euston Road.

A PRACTICAL MAN. I dessay it's a fine collection, enough, but it's a pity the things ain't more perfect. *I* should ha' thought, with so many odds and ends and rubbish lying about as is no use to nobody at present they might ha' used it up in mending some that only requires a 'arm 'ere or a leg there, or a 'ed and what not, to make 'em as good as ever. But ketch *them* (*he means the Officials*) taking any extra trouble if they can help it !

HIS COMPANION. Ah, but yer see it ain't so easy fitting on bits that belonged to something different. You've got to look at it *that* way.

THE P. M. *I* don't see no difficulty about it. Why, any stonemason could cut down the odd pieces to fit well enough, and they wouldn't have such a neglected appearance as they do now.

A Group has collected round a Gigantic Arm in red granite.

FIRST SIGHTSEER. There's a *arm* for yer !

SECOND S. (*a humourist*). Yes ; 'ow would yer like to 'ave *that* come a punching your 'ed ?

THIRD S. (*thoughtfully*). I expect they've put it up 'ere as a sarmple like.

THE MORALIZING MATRON. How it makes one realize that there were giants in those days !

HER FRIEND. But surely the size must be a *little* exaggerated, don't you think ? Oh, is *this* the God Ptah ?

> [*The M. M. says nothing, but clicks her tongue to express a grieved pity, after which she passes on.*

THE INTELLIGENT ARTISAN *and his* FIANCÉE *have entered the Nineveh Gallery, and are regarding an immense human-headed, winged bull.*

THE I. A. (*indulgently*). Rum-looking sort o' beast that 'ere.

FIANCÉE. Ye-es—I wonder if it's a likeness of some animal they used to 'ave then ?

THE I. A. I *did* think you was wider than *that !*—it's only imaginative. What 'ud be the good o' wings to a bull ?

FIANCÉE (*on her defence*). You think you know so much—but it's got a man's 'ed, ain't it? and I know there used to be *'orses* with 'alf a man where the 'ed ought to be, because I've seen their pictures— so there!

THE I. A. I dunno what you've got where *your* 'ed ought to be, torking such rot!

IN THE UPPER GALLERIES; ETHNOGRAPHICAL COLLECTION.

THE GRIM GOVERNESS (*directing a scared small boy's attention to a particularly hideous mask*). See, Henry, that's the kind of mask worn by savages!

HENRY. Always—or only on the fifth of November, Miss Goole?

> [*He records a mental vow never to visit a Savage Island on Guy Fawkes's Day, and makes a prolonged study of the mask, with a view to future nightmares.*

A KIND, BUT DENSE UNCLE (*to* NIECE). All these curious things were made by cannibals, ETHEL—savages who eat one another, you know.

ETHEL (*suggestively*). But, I suppose, Uncle, they wouldn't eat one another if they had any one to give them *buns*, would they?

> [*Her* UNCLE *discusses the suggestion elaborately, but without appreciating the hint; the* GOVERNESS *has caught sight of a huge and hideous Hawaiian Idol, with a furry orange-coloured head, big mother-o'-pearl eyes, with black balls for the pupils, and a grinning mouth picked out with shark's teeth, to which she introduces the horrified* HENRY.

MISS GOOLE. Now, Henry, you see the kind of idol the poor savages say their prayers to.

HARRY (*tremulously*). But n—not just before they go to bed, do they, Miss Goole?

AMONG THE MUMMIES.

THE UNCLE. That's King Rameses' mummy, Ethel.

ETHEL. And what was *her* name, Uncle?

THE GOVERNESS (*halting before a case containing a partially unrolled mummy, the spine and thigh of which are exposed to view).* Fancy, Henry, that's part of an Egyptian who has been dead for thousands of years! Why, you're not *frightened*, are you?

HARRY (*shaking*). No, I'm not frightened, Miss Goole—only if you don't mind, I—I'd rather see a gentleman not *quite* so dead. And there's one over there with a gold face and glass eyes, and he looked at me, and —please, I *don't* think this is the place to bring such a little boy as me to!

A Party is examining a Case of Mummied Animals.

THE LEADER. Here you are, you see, mummy cats—don't they look comical all stuck up in a row there?

FIRST WOMAN. Dear, dear—to think o' going to all that expense when they might have had 'em stuffed on a cushion! And monkeys, and dogs too—well, I'm sure, fancy *that* now!

SECOND WOMAN. And there's a mummied crocodile down there. I *don't* see what they'd want with a mummy *crocodile*, do you?

THE LEADER (*with an air of perfect comprehension of Egyptian customs*). Well, you see they took whatever they could get 'old of, *they* did.

IN THE PREHISTORIC GALLERY.

OLD LADY (*to* POLICEMAN) Oh, Policeman, can you tell me if there's any article here that's supposed to have belonged to Adam?

POLICEMAN (*a wag in his way*). Well, Mum, we '*ave* 'ad the 'andle of his spade, and the brim of his garden 'at, but they wore out last year and 'ad to be thrown away—things won't last for ever—even '*ere*, you know.

GOING OUT.

A PEEVISH OLD MAN. I ain't seen anything to call worth seeing, *I* ain't. In our Museum at 'ome they've a lamb with six legs, and hairy-light stones as big as cannon-balls; but there ain't none of that sort 'ere, and I'm dog-tired trapesing over these boards, I am!

His Daughter (*a candid person*). Ah, I ought to ha' known it warn't much good taking *you* out to enjoy yourself—you're too old, *you* are!

Ethel's Uncle (*cheerily*). Well, Ethel, I think we've seen all there is to be seen, eh?

Ethel. There's *one* room we haven't been into yet, Uncle, dear.

Uncle. Ha—and what's that?

Ethel (*persuasively*). The *Refreshment* Room.

[*The hint is accepted at last.*

The Travelling Menagerie.

OUTSIDE.

*A crowd is staring stolidly at the gorgeously gilded and painted entrance,
with an affectation of superior wisdom to that of the weaker-minded,
who sneak apologetically up the steps from time to time. A tall-hatted
orchestra have just finished a tune, and hung their brazen instruments
up like joints on the hooks above them.*

A WOMAN CARRYING AN INFANT (*to her* HUSBAND). Will 'ee goo in,
Joe?

JOE (*who is secretly burning to see the show*). Naw. Sin it arl afoor
arfen enough. Th' outside's th' best on it, I reckon.

HIS WIFE (*disappointed*). Saw 'tis, and naw charge for lookin' at 'en
neither.

THE PROPRIETOR. Ladies and Gentlemen, Re-mem-bar! This is
positively the last opportunity of witnessing Denman's Celebrated
Menagerie—the largest in the known world! The Lecturer is now
describing the animals, after which Mlle. Cravache and Zambango, the
famous African Lion-tamers, will go through their daring feats with
forest-bred lions, tigers, bears, and hyenas, for the last time in this town.
Remembar—the last performance this evening!

JOE (*to his* WIFE). If ye'd *like* to hev a look at 'em, I wun't say nay to et.

HIS WIFE. I dunno as I care partickler 'bout which way 'tis.

JOE (*annoyed*). Bide where 'ee be then.

HIS WIFE. Theer's th' child, Joe, to be sure.

JOE. Well we bain't a gooin' in, and so th' child wun't come to no
'arm, and theer's a hend on it!

His Wife. Nay, she'd lay in my arms as quiet as quiet. I wur on'y thinkin', Joe, as it 'ud be somethin' to tell her when she wur a big gell, as her daddy took her to see th' wild beasties afoor iver she could tark— that's arl I wur meanin', Joe. And they'll let 'er goo in free, too.

Joe. Ay, that'll be fine tellin's fur 'er, sure 'nough. Come arn, Missus, we'll tek th' babby in—happen she'll niver git th' chance again.

[*They mount the steps eagerly.*

INSIDE.

Joe's Wife (*with a vague sense of being defrauded*). I thart thee'rd ha' bin moor smell, wi' so many on 'em!

Joe. They doan't git naw toime for it, I reckon, allus on the rord as they be.

The Lecturer. Illow me to request yar kind hattention for a moment. (Stand back there, you boys, and don't beyave in such a silly manner!) We har now arrived at the Haswail, or Sloth Bear, described by Buffon as 'aving 'abits which make it a burden to itself. (*Severely.*) The Haswail. In the hajoinin' cage observe the Loocorricks, the hony hanimal to oom fear is habsolootly hunknown. When hattacked by the Lion, he places his 'ed between his fore-legs, and in that position awaits the honset of his would-be destroyer.

Joe's Wife. I thart it wur th' *hostridge* as hacted that away.

Joe. Ostridges ain't gotten they long twisted harns as iver *I* heard on.

His Wife (*stopping before another den*). Oh, my blessed! 'Ere be a queer-lookin' critter, do 'ee look at 'en, Joe. What'll *he* be now?

Joe. How do 'ee suppose as I be gooin' to tell 'ee the name of 'en? He'll likely be a sart of a 'arse. [*Dubiously.*

His Wife. They've a let' en git wunnerful ontidy fur sure. 'Ere, Mister (*to* Stranger) can you tell us the name of that theer hanimal?

Stranger. That—oh, that's a Gnu.

Joe's Wife. He says it be a noo.

Joe. A noo *what?*

His Wife. Why, a noo *hanimal,* I s'pose.

JOE. Well, he bain't naw himprovement on th' hold 'uns, as I can see. They'd better ha' left it aloan if they couldn't do naw better nor '*im*. Dunno what things be coming to, hinventin' o' noo hanimals at this time o' day.

BEFORE ANOTHER CAGE.

A BOOZED AND ARGUMENTATIVE RUSTIC. I sez as that 'un's a fawks, an' I'm ready to prove it on anny man.

A COMPANION (*soothingly*). Naw, naw, 'e baint naw fawks. I dunno what 'tis,—but 'tain't naw fawks nawhow.

B. AND A. RUSTIC. I tell 'ee '*tis* a fawks, I'm sure on it. (*To* MILD VISITOR) *Bain't* 'e a fawks, Master, eh?

MILD VISITOR. Well, really, if you ask me, I should say it was a hyena.

THE RUSTIC'S COMP. A hyanna! ah, that's a deal moor like; saw 'tis!

THE RUSTIC. A pianner? Do 'ee take me vur a vool? I'll knack th' 'ed arf o' the man as plays 'is priskies wi' me, I wull! Wheer be 'e? Let me get at 'en!

      [MILD V. *not being prepared to defend his opinion by personal combat, discreetly loses himself in crowd.*

ON THE ELEPHANT'S BACK.

SECOND BOY. Sit a bit moor forrard, Billy, cann't 'ee!

FIRST BOY. *Cann't*, I tell 'ee, I be sittin' on th' scruff of 'is neck as 'tis.

THIRD BOY. I can see my vaither, I can. 'Ere, vaither, vaither, look at me—see wheer *I* be!

FOURTH BOY (*a candid friend*). Shoot oop, cann't 'ee', ya young gozzle-'ead! Think ya vaither niver see a hass on a hellyphant afoor!

FIFTH BOY. These yere helliphants be main straddly roidin'. I wish 'e wudn't waak honly waun haff of 'en at oncest, loike. What do 'ee mean, a kitchin' old o' me behind i' that way, eh, Jimmy Passons!

"I SEZ AS THAT UN'S A FAWKS, AN' I'M READY TO PROVE IT ON ANNY MAN."

SIXTH BOY. *You'd* ketch 'old 'o hanything if you was like me, a slidin' down th' helliphant's ta-ail.

FIFTH BOY. If 'ee doan't let go o' me, I'll job th' helliphant's ribs, and make 'un gallop, I will, so *now*, Jimmy Passons!

IN FRONT OF THE LIONS' DEN DURING PERFORMANCE.

VARIOUS SPEAKERS. Wheer be pushin' to? Car that manners screouging like that! . . . I cann't see nawthen, *I* cann't wi' all they 'ats in front . . . What be gooin' arn, do 'ee know? . . . A wumman gooin' in along 'o they lions and tigerses? Naw, ye niver mane it! . . . Bain't she a leatherin' of 'un too! . . . Now she be a kissin' of 'un—maakin' it oop loike. . . . John, you can see better nor me—what be she oop to now? . . . Puttin' 'er 'ed inside o' th' lion's? Aw, dear me, now—*there's* a thing to be doin' of! Well, I'd ruther it was 'er nor me, I know *that* . . . They wun't do 'er naw 'arm, so long's she kips 'er heye on 'em . . . What do 'ee taak so voolish vor? How's th' wumman to kip 'er heye on 'em, with 'er 'ed down wan on 'em's throat, eh? . . . Gracious alive! if iver I did! . . . Oh, I do 'ope she bain't gooin' to let off naw fire-arms, I be moor fear'd o' pistols nor any tigers . . . Theer, she's out now! She be bold fur a female, bain't her? . . . She niver maade 'em joomp through naw bla-azin' 'oops, though. . . . What carl would she hev fur doin' that? Well, they've a drared 'er doin' of it houtside', that's arl I know . . . An' they've a drared Hadam outside a naamin' of th' hanimals—but ye didn't expect to see *that* doon inside', did 'ee? . . . Bob, do 'ee look at old Muster Manders ovver theer by th' hellyphant. He's a maakin' of 'isself that familiar— putting biskuts 'tween his lips and lettin' th' hellyphant take 'em out wi's troonk! . . . *I* see un—let un aloan, th' hold doitler, happen he thinks he's a feedin' his canary bird!

At the Regent Street Tussaud's.

Before the effigy of Dr. Koch, who is represented in the act of examining a test-tube with the expression of bland blamelessness peculiar to Wax Models.

WELL-INFORMED VISITOR. That's Dr. Koch, making his great discovery!

UNSCIENTIFIC V. What did *he* discover?

WELL-INF. V. Why, the Consumption Bacillus. He's got it in that bottle he's holding up.

UNSC. V. And what's the good of it, now he *has* discovered it?

WELL-INF. V. Good? Why, it's the thing that causes *consumption*, you know!

UNSC. V. Then it's a pity he didn't leave it alone!

Before a Scene representing " The Home Life at Sandringham."

FIRST OLD LADY (*with Catalogue*). It says here that " the note the page is handing *may* have come from Sir Dighton Probyn, the Comptroller of the Royal Household." Fancy *that!*

SECOND OLD LADY. He's brought it in in his fingers. Now *that's* a thing I never allow in *my* house. I always tell Sarah to bring all letters, and even circulars, in on a tray!

Before a Scene representing the late Fred Archer, on a rather quaint quadruped, on Ascot Racecourse.

A SPORTSMAN. H'm—Archer, eh? Shouldn't have backed his mount in *that* race!

Before " The Library at Hawarden."

GLADSTONIAN ENTHUSIAST (*to* FRIEND, *who, with the perverse ingenuity of patrons of Waxworks, has been endeavouring to identify the Rev. John Wesley among the Cabinet in Downing Street*). Oh, never mind all that lot, Betsy ; they're only the *Gover'ment !* Here's dear Mr. and Mrs. Gladstone in this next ! See, he's lookin' for something in a drawer of his side-board—ain't that *natural ?* And only look—a lot of people have been leaving Christmas cards on him (*a pretty and touching tribute of affection, which is eminently characteristic of a warm-hearted Public*). I wish I'd thought o' bringing one with me !

HER FRIEND. So do I. We might send one 'ere by post—but it'll have to be a New Year Card now !

A STRICT OLD LADY (*before next group*). Who are these two ? " Mr. 'Enery Irving, and Miss Ellen Terry in *Faust*, eh ? No—I don't care to stop to see them—that's play-actin', that is—and I don't 'old with it no-how ! What are these two parties supposed to be doin' of over here ? What—Cardinal Newman and Cardinal Manning at the High Altar at the Oratory, Brompton ! Come along, and don't encourage Popery by looking at such figures. I *did* 'ear as they'd got Mrs. Pearcey and the prambilator somewheres. I *should* like to see that, now.

IN THE CHILDREN'S GALLERY.

AN AUNT (*who finds the excellent Catalogue a mine of useful informa-tion*). Look, Bobby, dear (*reading*). " Here we have Constantine's Cat, as seen in the *Nights of Straparola*, an Italian romancist, whose book was translated into French in the year 1585—"

BOBBY (*disappointed*). Oh, then it *isn't Puss in Boots !*

A GENIAL GRANDFATHER (*pausing before Crusoe and Friday*). Well, Percy, my boy, you know who *that* is, at all events—eh ?

PERCY. I suppose it is Stanley—but it's not very like.

THE G. G. Stanley !—Why, bless my soul, never heard of *Robinson Crusoe* and his man *Friday ?*

PERCY. Oh, I've *heard* of them, of course—they come in Pantomimes

"THAT'S PLAY-ACTIN', THAT IS—AND I DON'T 'OLD WITH IT NOHOW!"

—but I like more grown-up sort of books myself, you know. Is this girl asleep *She?*

THE G. G. No—at least—well, I expect it's *The Sleeping Beauty.*

You remember her, of course—all about the ball, and the glass slipper, and her father picking a rose when the hedge grew round the palace, eh?

PERCY. Ah, you see, Grandfather, you had more time for general reading than we get. (*He looks through a practicable cottage window.*) Hallo, a Dog and a Cat. Not badly stuffed!

THE G. G. Why, that must be *Old Mother Hubbard*. (*Quoting from memory.*) "Old Mother Hubbard sat in a cupboard, eating a Christmas pie—or a *bone* was it?"

PERCY. Don't know. It's not in *Selections from British Poetry*, which we have to get up for "rep."

THE AUNT (*reading from Catalogue*). "The absurd ambulations of this antique person, and the equally absurd antics of her dog, need no recapitulation." Here's *Jack the Giant Killer*, next. Listen, Bobby, to what it says about him here. (*Reads.*) "It is clearly the last transmutation of the old British legend told by Geoffrey of Monmouth, of Corineus, the Trojan, the companion of the Trojan Brutus, when he first settled in Britain. But more than this "—I hope you're listening, Bobby?—"*more* than this, it is quite evident, even to the superficial student of Greek mythology, that many of the main incidents and ornaments are borrowed from the tales of Hesiod and Homer." Think of that, now!

[BOBBY *thinks of it, with depression.*

THE G. G. (*before figure of Aladdin's Uncle selling new lamps for old*). Here you are, you see! "*Ali Baba*," got 'em all here, you see. Never read your *Arabian Nights*, either! Is that the way they bring up boys nowadays!

PERCY. Well, the fact is, Grandfather, that unless a fellow reads that kind of thing when he's *young*, he doesn't get a chance afterwards.

THE AUNT (*still quoting*). "In the famous work," Bobby, "by which we know Masûdi, he mentions the Persian Hezar Afsane-um-um-um,—nor have commentators failed to notice that the occasion of the book written for the Princess Homai resembles the story told in the Hebrew Bible about Esther, her mother or grandmother, by some Persian Jew two or three centuries B.C." Well, I never knew *that* before! . . . This is *Sindbad and the Old Man of the Sea*—let's see what they say about *him*.

(*Reads.*) "Both the story of *Sindbad* and the old Basque legend of Tartaro are undoubtedly borrowed from the *Odyssey* of Homer, whose *Iliad* and *Odyssey* were translated into Syriac in the reign of Harun-ur-Rashid." Dear, dear, how interesting, now! and, Bobby, what *do* you think some one says about *Jack and the Beanstalk?* He says—"This tale is an allegory of the Teutonic Al-fader, the red hen representing the all-producing sun; the moneybags, the fertilizing rain; and the harp, the winds." Well, I'm sure it seems likely enough, doesn't it?

[BOBBY *suppresses a yawn;* PERCY'S *feelings are outraged by receiving a tin trumpet from the Lucky Tub; general move to the scene of the Hampstead Tragedy.*

BEFORE THE HAMPSTEAD TABLEAUX.

SPECTATORS. Dear, dear, there's the *dresser*, you see, and the window broken and all; it's wonderful how they can *do* it! And there's poor Mrs. 'Ogg—it's real butter and a real loaf she's cutting, and the poor baby, too! . . . Here's the actual casts taken after they were murdered. Oh, and there's Mrs. Pearcey wheeling the perambulator—it's the *very* perambulator! No, not the very one—they've got *that* at the other place, and the piece of toffee the baby sucked. Have they really! Oh, we *must* try and go there, too, before the children's holidays are over. And this is all? Well, well, everything very nice, I *will* say. But a pity they couldn't get the *real* perambulator!

At the Military Exhibition.

IN THE AVENUE FACING THE ARENA.

AN UNREASONABLE OLD LADY (*arriving breathless, with her grand-son and niece*). This'll be the place the balloon goes up from, I wouldn't miss it for anything! Put the child up on that bench, Maria; we'll stand about here till it begins.

MARIA. But *I* don't see no balloon nor nothing.

[*Which, as the foliage blocks out all but the immediate foreground is scarcely surprising.*

THE U. O. L. No more don't I—but it stands to reason there wouldn't be so many looking on if there wasn't *something* to see. We're well enough where we are, and *I'm* not going further to fare worse to please nobody; so you may do as you *like* about it.

[MARIA *promptly avails herself of this permission.*

THE U. O. L. (*a little later*). Well, it's time they did *something*, I'm sure. Why, the people seem all moving off! and where's that girl Maria got to? Ah, here you are! So you found you were no better off?—*Next* time, p'raps you'll believe what I tell you. Not that there's any War Balloon as *I* can see!

MARIA. Oh, there was a capital view from where *I* was—out in the open there.

THE U. O. L. Why couldn't you say so before? Out in the open! Let's go there then—it's all the same to *me*!

MARIA (*with an undutiful giggle*). It's all the same now—wherever you go, 'cause the balloon's gone up.

THE U. O. L. Gone up! What are you telling me, Maria?

MARIA. I see it go—it shot up ever so fast and quite steady, and the people in the car all waved their 'ats to us. I could see a arm a waving almost till it got out of sight.

THE U. O. L. And me and this innercent waiting here on the seat like lambs, and never dreaming what was goin' on! Oh, Maria, however you'll reconcile it to your conscience, *I* don't know!

MARIA. Why, whatever are you pitching into *me* for!

THE U. O. L. It's not that it's any partickler pleasure to *me*, seeing a balloon, though we *did* get our tea done early to be in time for it—it's the sly deceitfulness of your *conduck*, Maria, which is all the satisfaction I get for coming out with you,—it's the feeling that—well, there, I won't *talk* about it!

> [*In pursuance of which virtuous resolve, she talks about nothing else for the remainder of the day, until the unfortunate* MARIA *wishes fervently that balloons had never been invented.*]

IN THE BUILDING.

An admiring group has collected before an enormous pin-cushion in the form of a fat star, and about the size of a Church-hassock.

FIRST SOLDIER (*to his Companion*). Lot 'o work in *that*, yer know!

SECOND SOLDIER. Yes. (*Thoughtfully.*) Not but what—(*becoming critical*)—if I'd been doin' it *myself*, I should ha' chose pins with smaller 'eds on 'em.

FIRST S. (*regarding this as presumptuous*). You may depend on it the man who made *that* 'ad his reasons for choosing the pins he did—but there's no pleasing some parties!

SECOND S. (*apologetically*). Well, I ain't denying the *Art* in it, am I?

FIRST WOMAN. I *do* call that 'andsome, Sarah. See, there's a star, and two 'arps, and a crownd, and I don't know what all—and all done in pins and beads! "Made by Bandsman Brown," too! [*Reading placard.*

SECOND W. Soldiers is that clever with their 'ands. Four pounds seems a deal to ask for it, though.

FIRST W. But look at the weeks it must ha' took him to do! (*Reading.*)

"Containing between ten and eleven thousand pins and beads, and a hundred and ninety-eight pieces of coloured cloth!" Why, the pins alone must ha' cost a deal of money.

SECOND W. Yes, it 'ud be a pity for it to go to somebody as 'ud want to take 'em out.

FIRST W. It ought to be bought up by Gover'ment, that it ought—they're well able to afford it.

A select party of Philistines, comprising a young Man, apparently in the Army, and his MOTHER and SISTER, are examining Mr. Gilbert's Jubilee Trophy in a spirit of puzzled antipathy.

THE MOTHER. Dear me, and *that's* the Jubilee centrepiece, is it? What a heavy-looking thing. I wonder what *that* cost?

HER SON (*gloomily*). Cost? Why, about two days' pay for every man in the Service!

HIS MOTHER. Well, I call it a shame for the Army to be fleeced for *that* thing. Are those creatures intended for mermaids, with their tails curled round that glass ball, I wonder? [*She sniffs.*

HER DAUGHTER. I expect it will be crystal, Mother.

HER MOTHER. Very likely, my dear, but—glass or crystal—*I* see no sense in it!

DAUGHTER. Oh, it's absurd, of course—still, this figure isn't badly done. Is it supposed to represent St. George carrying the Dragon? Because they've made the Dragon no bigger than a salmon!

MOTHER. Ah, well, I hope Her Majesty will be better pleased with it than I am, that's all.

> [*After which they fall into ecstasies over an industrial exhibit consisting of a drain-pipe, cunningly encrusted with fragments of regimental mess-china set in gilded cement.*

Before a large mechanical clock, representing a fortress, which is striking. Trumpets sound, detachments of wooden soldiers march in and out of gateways, and parade the battlements, clicking for a considerable time.

A SPECTATOR (*with a keen sense of the fitness of things*). What—all that for on'y 'alf past five!

OVERHEARD IN THE AMBULANCE DEPARTMENT.

SPECTATORS (*passing in front of groups of models arranged in realistic surroundings*).   All the faces screwed up to suffering, you see ! . . . What a nice patient expression that officer on the stretcher has ! Yes, they've given *him* a wax head—some of them are only *papier-mâché.* . . . Pity they couldn't get nearer their right size in 'elmets, though, ain't it ? . . . There's *one* chap's given up the ghost ! . . . I know that stuffed elephant —he comes from the Indian Jungle at the Colinderies ! . . . I *do* think it's a pity they couldn't get something more *like* a mule than this wooden thing ! Why, it's quite *flat,* and its ears are only leather, nailed on ! . . . You can't tell, my dear ; it may be a peculiar breed out there—cross between a towel-horse and a donkey-engine, don't you know !

IN THE INDIAN JUNGLE SHOOTING-GALLERY.

At the back, amidst tropical scenery, an endless procession of remarkably undeceptive rabbits of painted tin are running rapidly up and down an inclined plane. Birds jerk painfully through the air above, and tin rats, boars, tigers, lions, and ducks, all of the same size, glide swiftly along grooves in the middle distance. In front, Commissionnaires are busy loading rifles for keen sportsmen, who keep up a lively but somewhat ineffective fusillade.

'ARRIET (*to* 'ARRY). They 'ave got it up beautiful, I must say. Do you *get* anything for 'itting them ?

'ARRY. On'y the honour.

A FATHER (*to intelligent* SMALL BOY *in rear of* NERVOUS SPORTSMAN). No, I ain't seen him 'it anything *yet,* my son ; but you watch. That's a rabbit he's aiming at now. . . . Ah, *missed* him !

SMALL BOY. 'Ow d'yer *know* what the gentleman's a-aiming at, eh, Father ?

FATHER. 'Ow ? Why, you notice which way he points his gun.

[*The N. S. fires again—without results.*

SMALL BOY. I sor that time, Father. He was a-aiming at one o' them ducks, an' he missed a rabbit !   [*The N. S. gives it up in disgust.*

" GO IN, JIM ! YOU GOT YER MARKIN'-PAPER READY ANYHOW."

Enter a small party of 'Arries in high spirits.

FIRST 'ARRY. 'Ullo ! *I*'m on to this. 'Ere Guv'nor', 'and us a gun. *I*'ll show yer 'ow to shoot !

[*He takes up his position, in happy unconsciousness that playful companions have decorated his coat-collar behind with a long piece of white paper.*

SECOND 'ARRY. Go in, Jim! You got yer markin'-paper ready anyhow.

[*Delighted guffaws from the other* 'ARRIES, *in which* JIM *joins vaguely.*

THIRD 'ARRY. I'll lay you can't knock a rabbit down!

JIM. I'll lay I can!

[*Fires. The procession of rabbits goes on undisturbed.*

SECOND 'ARRY (*jocosely*). Never mind. You *peppered* 'im. I sor the feathers floy!

THIRD 'ARRY. You'd ha' copped 'im if yer'd bin a bit quicker.

JIM (*annoyed*). They keep on movin' so, they don't give a bloke no chornce!

SECOND 'ARRY. 'Ave a go at that old owl.

[*Alluding to a tin representation of that fowl which remains stationary among the painted rushes.*

THIRD 'ARRY. No—see if you can't git that stuffed bear. He's on'y a yard or two away!

AN IMPATIENT 'ARRY (*at doorway*). 'Ere, *come on!* Ain't you shot enough? Shake a leg, can't yer, Jim?

SECOND 'ARRY. He's got to kill one o' them rabbits fust. Or pot a tin lion, Jim? *You* ain't afraid?

JIM. No ; I'm goin' to git that owl. 'He's *quiet* any way.

[*Fires. The owl falls prostrate.*

SECOND 'ARRY. Got 'im! Owl's *orf!* Jim, old man, you must stand drinks round after this!

[*Exeunt* 'ARRIES, *to celebrate their victory in a befitting fashion, as Scene closes in.*

At the French Exhibition.

CHORUS OF ARAB STALL-KEEPERS. Come an look! Alaha-ba-li-boo! Ect is verri cold to-day! I-ah-rish Brandi! 'Ere *Miss!* you com' 'ere! No pay for lookin'. Alf a price! Verri pritti, verri nah-ice, verri cheap verri moch! [*And so on.*]

CHORUS OF BRITISH SALESWOMEN. *Will* you allow me to show you this little novelty, Sir? 'Ave you seen the noo perfume sprinkler? Do come and try this noo puzzle—no 'arm in *lookin'*, Sir. Very nice little novelties 'ere, Sir! 'Eard the noo French Worltz, Sir? every article is very much reduced, &c., &c.

AT THE FOLIES-BERGÈRE.

SCENE—*A hall in the grounds. Several turnstiles leading to curtained entrances.*

SHOWMAN (*shouting*). Amphitrite, the Marvellous Floatin' Goddess Just about to commence! This way for the Mystic Gallery—three illusions for threepence! Atalanta, the Silver Queen of the Moon; the Oriental Beauty in the Table of the Sphinx, and the Wonderful Galatea, or Pygmalion's Dream. Only threepence! This way for the Mystic Marvel o' She! Now commencing!

A FEMALE SIGHTSEER (*with the air of a person making an original suggestion*). Shall we go in, just to see what it's like?

MALE DITTO. May as well, now we *are* 'ere. (*To preserve*

I.

"COME AN LOOK! ALAHA-BA-LI-BOO!"

himself from any suspicion of credulity). Sure to be a take-in o' some sort.

> [*They enter a dim apartment, in which two or three people are leaning over a barrier in front of a small Stage ; the Curtain is lowered, and a Pianist is industriously pounding away at a Waltz.*

THE F. S. (*with an uncomfortable giggle*). Not much to see *so* far, is there ?

HER COMPANION. Well, they ain't begun yet.

> [*The Waltz ends, and the Curtain rises, disclosing a* CAVERN SCENE. AMPHITRITE, *in blue tights, rises through the floor.*

AMPHITRITE (*in the Gallic tongue*). Mesdarms et Messures, j'ai l'honnoor de vous sooayter le bong jour ! (*Floats, with no apparent support, in the air, and performs various graceful evolutions, concluding by reversing herself completely.*) Bong swore, Mesdarms et messures, mes remercimongs !

> [*She dives below, and the Curtain descends.*

THE F. S. Is that all ? I don't see nothing in *that !*

HER COMP. (*who, having paid for admission, resents this want of appreciation*). Why, she was off the ground the 'ole of the time, wasn't she ? I'd just like to see *you* turnin' and twisting about in the air as easy as she did with nothing to 'old on by !

THE F. S. I didn't notice she was off the ground—yes that *was* clever. I never thought o' that before. Let's go and see the other things now.

HER COMP. Well, if you don't see nothing surprising in 'em till they're all over, you might as well stop outside, *I* should ha' thought.

THE F. S. Oh, but I'll notice more next time—you've got to get *used* to these things, you know.

> [*They enter the Mystic Gallery, and find themselves in a dim passage, opposite a partitioned compartment, in which is a glass case, supported on four pedestals, with a silver crescent at the back. The illusions—to judge from a sound of scurrying behind the scenes—have apparently been taken somewhat unawares.*

THE FEMALE SIGHTSEER (*anxious to please*). They've done that 'alf-moon very well, haven't they ?

VOICE OF SHOWMAN (*addressing the Illusions*). Now then, 'urry up there—we're all waiting for you.

> [*The face of " Atalanta, the Silver Queen of the Moon," appears strongly illuminated, inside the glass-box, and regards the spectators with an impassive contempt—greatly to their confusion.*

THE MALE S. (*in a propitiatory tone*). Not a bad-looking girl, is she ?

ATALANTA, THE QUEEN OF THE MOON (*to the* ORIENTAL BEAUTY *in next compartment*). Polly, when these people are gone, I wish you'd fetch me my work !

> [*The Sightseers move on, feeling crushed. In the second compartment the upper portion of a female is discovered, calmly knitting in the centre of a small table, the legs of which are distinctly visible.*

THE FEMALE S. Why, wherever has the *rest* of her got to ?

THE ORIENTAL BEAUTY (*with conscious superiority*). That's what you've got to find out.

> [*They pass on to interview "Galatea, or Pygmalion's Dream," whose compartment is as yet enveloped in obscurity.*

A YOUTHFUL SHOWMAN (*apparently on familiar terms with all the Illusions*). Ladies and Gentlemen, I shell now 'ave the honour of persentin' to you the wonderful Galatear or Livin' Statue ; you will 'ave an oppertoonity of 'andling the bust for yourselves, which will warm before your eyes into living flesh, and the lovely creecher live and speak. 'Ere, look sharp, carn't yer ! (*To* GALATEA.)

PYGMALION'S DREAM (*from the Mystic gloom*). Wait a bit till I've done warming my 'ands. Now you can turn the lights up . . . there, you've bin and turned 'em *out* now, stoopid !

THE Y. S. Don't you excite yourself. I know what I'm doin'. (*Turns the lights up, and reveals a large terra-cotta Bust.*) At my request, this young lydy will now perceed to assoom the yew and kimplexion of life itself. Galatear, will you oblige us by kindly coming to life ?

> [*The Bust vanishes, and is replaced by a decidedly earthly Young Woman in robust health.*

THE Y. S. Thenk you. That's all I wanted of yer. Now, will you kindly return to your former styte ?

> [*The Young Woman transforms herself into a hideous Skull.*

THE Y. S. (*in a tone of remonstrance*). No—no, not that ridiklous fice ! We don't want to see what yer will be—it's very *loike* yer, I know but still—(*the skull changes to the Bust.*) Ah, that's more the stoyle ! (*Takes the Bust by the neck and hands it round for inspection.*) And now, thenking you for your kind attention, and on'y 'orskin one little fyvour of you, that is, that you will not reveal 'ow it is done, I will now bid you a very good evenin', Lydies and Gentlemen !

THE F. S. (*outside*). It's wonderful how they can do it all for three-pence, isn't it ? We haven't seen *She* yet !

HER COMP. What ! 'aven't you seen wonders enough ? Come on, then. But you *are* going it you know !

> [*They enter a small room, at the further end of which are a barrier and proscenium with drawn hangings.*

THE EXHIBITOR (*in a confidential tone, punctuated by bows*). I will not keep you waiting, Ladies and Gentlemen, but at once proceed with a few preliminary remarks. Most of you, no doubt, have read that celebrated story by Mr. Rider 'Aggard, about a certain *She-who-must-be-obeyed*, and who dwelt in a place called Kôr, and you will also doubtless remember how she was in the 'abit of repairing at certain intervals, to a cavern, and renooing her youth in a fiery piller. On one occasion, wishing to indooce her lover to foller her example, she stepped into the flame to encourage him—something went wrong with the works, and she was instantly redooced to a cinder. I fortunately 'appened to be near at the time (you will escuse a little wild fib from a showman, I'm sure !) I 'appened to be porsin by, and was thus enabled to secure the ashes of the Wonderful SHE, which—(*draws hangings and reveals a shallow metal Urn suspended in the centre of scene*) are now before you enclosed in that little urn. She—where are you?

SHE (*in a full sweet voice from below*). I am 'ere!

SHOWMAN. Then appear!

[*The upper portion of an exceedingly comely* YOUNG PERSON *emerges from the mouth of the Urn.*

THE F. S. (*startled*). Lor, she give me quite a turn!

SHOWMAN. Some people think this is all done by mirrors, but it is not so ; it is managed by a simple arrangement of light and shade. She will now turn slowly round, to convince you that she is really inside the urn and not merely beyind it. (*She turns round condescendingly.*) She will next pass her 'ands completely round her, thereby demonstrating the utter impossibility of there being any wires to support her. Now she will rap on the walls on each side of her, proving to you that she is no reflection, but a solid reality, after which she will tap the bottom of the urn beneath her so that you may see it really is what it purports to be. (SHE *performs all these actions in the most obliging manner.*) She will now disappear for a moment. (SHE *sinks into the Urn.*) Are you still there, She?

SHE (*from the recess of the Urn*). Yes.

SHOWMAN. Then will you give us some sign of your presence? (*a hand and arm are protruded and waved gracefully*). Thank you. Now you can come up again. (SHE *reappears.*) She will now answer any questions any lady or gentleman may like to put to her, always provided you won't ask her how it is done—for I'm sure she wouldn't give me away, *would* you, She?

SHE (*with a slow bow and gracious smile*). Certingly not.

THE F. S. (*to her* COMPANION). Ask her something—do.

HER COMP. Go on! *I* ain't got anything to ask her—ask her yourself!

A BOLDER SPIRIT (*with interest*). Are your *feet* warm?

SHE. Quite—thenks.

THE SHOWMAN. How old are you, She?

SHE (*impressively*). Two theousand years.

'ARRY. And quite a young thing, too!

A SPECTATOR (*who has read the Novel*). 'Ave you 'eard from Leo Vincey lately ?

SHE (*coldly*). I don't know the gentleman.

SHOWMAN. If you have no more questions to ask her, She will now retire into her Urn thenking you all for your kind attendance this morning, which will conclude the entertainment.

> [*Final disappearance of* SHE. *The Audience pass out, feeling—with perfect justice—that they have "had their money's worth."*

In the Mall on Drawing-Room Day.

The line of carriages bound for Buckingham Palace is moving by slow stages down the Drive. A curious but not uncritical crowd, consisting largely of females, peer into the carriages as they pass, and derive an occult pleasure from a glimpse of a satin train and a bouquet. Other spectators circulate behind them, roving from carriage to carriage, straining and staring in at the occupants with the childlike interest of South Sea Islanders. The coachmen and footmen gaze impassively before them, ignoring the crowd to the best of their ability. The ladies in the carriages bear the ordeal of popular inspection with either haughty resignation elaborate unconsciousness, or amused tolerance, and it is difficult to say which demeanour provokes the greatest resentment in the democratic breast.

CHORUS OF FEMALE SPECTATORS. We shall see better here than what we did last Droring-Room. Law, 'ow it *did* come down, too, pouring the 'ole day. I was that sorry for the poor 'orses! . . . Oh, that one *was* nice, Marire! Did you see 'er train?—all flame-coloured satting—*lovely!* Ain't them flowers beautiful? Oh, Liza, 'ere's a pore skinny-lookin' thing coming next—look at 'er pore dear arms, all bare! But dressed 'andsome enough . . . That's a Gineral in there, see? He's 'olding his cocked 'at on his knee to save the feathers—him and her have been 'aving words, apparently . . . Oh, I *do* like this one. I s'pose that's her Mother with her—well, yes, o' course it *may* be her Aunt!

A SARDONIC LOAFER. 'Ullo, 'ere's a 'aughty one! layin' back and puttin' up 'er glorses! Know us agen, Mum, won't you? You may well look—you ain't seen so much in yer ole life as what you're seein' to-day, I'll lay! Ah, you ought to feel honoured, too, all of us comin' out to look

"OW, 'E SMOILED AT ME THROUGH THE BRORNCHES!"

at yer. Drored 'er blind down, this one 'as, yer see—knew she wasn't wuth looking at!

      [A carriage passes; the footman on the box is adorned by an
      enormous nosegay, over which he can just see.

    FIRST COMIC COCKNEY. Ow, I s'y—you 'ave come out in bloom, Johnny!

SECOND C. C. Ah, they've bin forcin' *'im* under glorse, they 'ave! 'Is Missis 'll never find 'im under all them flowers. Ow, 'e smoiled at me through the brornches!

> [*Another carriage passes, the coachman and footmen of which are undecorated.*

FIRST C. C. Shime!—they might ha' stood yer a penny bunch of voilets between yer, that they might!

THE SARDONIC L. 'Ere's a swell turn-out and no mistake—with a couple o' bloomin' beadles standin' be'ind! There's a full-fed 'un inside of it too,—look at the dimonds all over 'er bloomin' old nut. *My* eye! (*The elderly dowager inside produces a cut-glass scent-bottle of goodly size.*) Ah, she's got a drop o' the right sort in there—see her sniffin at it—it won't take 'er long to mop up that little lot!

JEAMES (*behind the carriage, to* CHAWLES). Our old geeser's per-doocin' the custimary amount o' sensation, eh, Chawley?

CHAWLES (*under notice*). Well, thank 'Eving, I sha'n't have to share the responsibility of her *much* longer!

'ARRIET (*to* ARRY). I wonder they don't get tired o' being stared at like they are.

'ARRY. Bless your 'art—*they* don't mind—they *like* it. They'll go 'ome and s'y (*in falsetto*) "Ow, Pa, all the bloomin' crowd kep' on a lookin' at us through the winder—it *was* proime!"

'ARRIET (*giggling admiringly*). 'Ow do *you* know the w'y they tork?

'ARRY (*superior*). Why, they don't tork partickler different from what you and me tork—do they?

FIRST MECHANIC. See all them old blokes in red, with the rum 'ats, Bill? They're Beefeaters goin' to the Pallis, they are.

SECOND M. What do they do when they git there?

FIRST M. Do? oh, mind the bloomin' staircase, and chuck out them as don' beyave themselves.

A RESTLESS LADY (*to her husband*). Harry, I don't like this place at all. I'm sure we could see better somewhere else. Do let's try and squeeze in somewhere lower down . . . No, this is worse—that *horrid* tobacco! Suppose we cross over to the Palace?   [*They do so.*

A POLICEMAN. Too late to cross now, Sir—go back, please.

> [*They go back and take up a position in front of the crowd on the curbstone.*

THE R. L. There, we shall see beautifully here, Harry.

A CRUSTY MATRON (*talking at the* R. L. *and her husband*). Well, I'm sure, some persons have got a cheek, coming in at the last minnit and standing in front of those that have stood here hours—that's ladylike, I *don't* think! Nor yet, I didn't come here to have my eye poked out by other parties' pairosols.

> [*Continues in this strain until the* R. L. *can stand it no longer, and urges her husband to depart.*

CHORUS OF POLICEMEN. Pass along there, please, one way *or* the other—keep moving there, Sir.

THE R. L. But where are we to *go*—we must stand *somewhere?*

A POLICEMAN. Can't stand anywhere 'ere, Mum.

> [*The unhappy couple are passed on from point to point, until they are finally hemmed in at a spot from which it is impossible to see anything whatever.*

HARRY. If you had only been content to stay where you were at first, we should have been all right!

THE R. L. Nonsense, it is all your fault, you *are* the most hopeless person to go anywhere with. Why didn't you tell one of those policemen *who we were?*

HARRY. Why? Well, because I didn't see one who looked as if it would interest him, if you want to know.

THE ROYAL CARRIAGES ARE APPROACHING.

CHORUS OF LOYAL LADIES OF VARIOUS AGES. There—they're clearing the way—the Prince and Princess won't be long now. Here's the Life Guards' Band—don't they look byootiful in those dresses? Won't that poor drummer's arms ache to-morrow? This is the escort coming now . . . 'Ere come the Royalties. Don't push so, Polly, you can see without that! . . . There, that was the Prince in the first one—did yer see

him, Polly?   Oh, yes, leastwise I see the end of a cocked 'at, which I took
to be 'im.   Yes, *that* was 'im right enough . . .   There goes the Princess—
wasn't she looking nice?   I couldn't exactly make out which was her and
which was the two young Princesses, they went by all in a flash like, but
they *did* look nice! . . . 'Ere's another Royalty in this kerridge—'oo will
she be, I wonder?   Oh, I expect it would be the old Duchess of——No, I
don't think it was *'er*,—she wasn't looking pleasant enough,—and she's
dead, too . . . Now they have got inside—'ark at them playing bits of
God Save the Queen.   Well, I'm glad I've seen it.

A SON (*to cheery old Lady*).   'Ow are you gettin' on, Mother, eh?

CH. O. L.   First-rate, thankee, John, my boy.

SON.   You ain't tired standing about so long?

CH. O. L.   Lor' bless you, no.   Don't you worry about *me.*

SON.   Could you see 'em from where you was?

CH. O. L.   I could see all the coachmen's 'ats beautiful.   We'll wait
and see 'em all come out, John, won't we?   They won't be more than an
hour and a half in there, I dessay.

A PERSON WITH A FLORID VOCABULARY.   Well, if I'd ha' known
all I was goin' to see was a set o' blanky nobs shut up in their blank-dash
kerridges, blank my blanky eyes if I'd ha' stirred a blanky foot, s'elp me
Dash, I wouldn't!

A VENDOR (*persuasively*).   The kerrect lengwidge of hevery flower
that blows—one penny!

At a Parisian Café Chantant.

SCENE—*An open air restaurant in the Champs-Elysées; the seats in the enclosure are rapidly filling; the diners in the gallery at the back have passed the salad stage, and are now free to take a more or less torpid interest in the Entertainment below. Enter* TWO BRITONS, *who make their way to a couple of vacant chairs close to the orchestra.*

FIRST BRITON. *Entrée libre*, you see; nothing to pay! Cheaper than your precious Exhibition, eh ?   [*Chuckles knowingly.*

SECOND BRITON (*who would rather have stayed at the Exhibition but doesn't like to say so*). Don't quite see how they expect the thing to pay if they don't charge anything, though.

FIRST B. Oh, they make *their* profit out of the dinners up in the gallery there.

SECOND B. (*appreciating the justice of this arrangement, having dined with his companion elsewhere*). Well, that's fair enough.

          [*Feels an increased respect for the Entertainment.*

FIRST B. Must get their money back somehow, you know. Capital seats for hearing, these. Now, we'll just take a cup of coffee, and a quiet cigar, while we listen to the singing—*you'll* enjoy this, *I* know !

        [*With the air of a man who knows the whole thing by heart; the Waiter brings two tumblers of black coffee, for which he demands the sum of six francs; lively indignation of the* TWO BRITONS, *who denounce the charge as a swindle, and take some time to recover sufficient equanimity to attend to what is going on on the Stage.*

FEMALE ARTISTE (SINGS REFRAIN).

FEMALE ARTISTE (*sings refrain*)—
>Pour notre Exposition,
>Il faut nous faire imposition ! &c., &c.

SECOND B. (*who not being at home in the language, rather resents his companion's laughter*). What's that she's saying ?

FIRST B. (*who laughed because he knew there was a joke about the Exhibition*). Eh ?—oh ! I'll tell you afterwards.

>[*Hopes his friend will have forgotten all about it by that time.*

SECOND B. (*pertinaciously, as the Singer kisses her hand, and rushes precipitately off stage*). Well, what was all *that* about ?

FIRST B. (*who, upon reflection, finds that he hasn't the faintest idea*). Oh, nothing very much—more the *manner*, you know, than anything else—it's the *men* who have all the really funny songs.

>[*A Male Artiste appears, bowing and kicking up his left leg behind : the* FIRST BRITON *bends forward with an anxious frown, determined to let nothing escape him this time. Fortunately, as* M. CHARLEMAGNE, *the Comic Singer, possesses a powerful voice, the* FIRST BRITON *is able to follow most of the words, from which, although they reach his ear in a somewhat perverted form, he contrives to extract intense amusement. This is how the Chanson reaches him :—*

>Seul boulevard silent vous arrête :
>Quand monde a tout départ n'amas,
>>[*He can't quite make out this last word.*
>Repondez vitement—
>>[*Something he doesn't catch.*
>Le fou l'eau sitôt vous crie "un rat !"
>[*Here he whispers to his friend that " That last line was rather neat."*

Refrain (*to which* M. CHARLEMAGNE *dances a gavotte with his hat thrust into the small of his back*).

>Il n'a pas départ Dinard.

>[*This makes the* FIRST BRITON—*who once spent a week at Dinard—laugh immoderately.*

Ne Pa, ne Ma! (*bis*)
C'était pas tant, mais sais comme ça—
Il n'a pas départ Dinard,
Il non a pas certain-y-mal là !

FIRST BRITON (*to Second Ditto*). *Very* funny, isn't he ?

SECOND B. (*who—less fortunate than his friend—has not caught a single word*). Um—can't say I see much in it myself.

FIRST B. (*compassionately*). Can't you ? Oh, you'll get into the way of it presently.

SECOND B. But what's the joke of all that about "Pa" ?

FIRST B. (*who has been honestly under the impression that he did see a point somewhere*). Why, he says he's an orphan—hasn't any Pa nor Ma.

SECOND B. (*captiously*). Well, there's nothing so very funny in *that !*

FIRST B. (*giving up the point on consideration, as* M. CHARLEMAGNE *skips off*). Oh, it's all nonsense, of course ; these fellows only come on to fill up the time till Pôlusse sings (*feels rather proud of having caught the right pronunciation*). Pôlusse is the only one really worth listening to.

SECOND B. (*watching two Niggers in a Knockabout Entertainment*). I can follow *these* chaps better. [*Complacently.*

One of the Niggers [*to the other*]. Ha, George Washington, Sar. I'll warm you fur dat ar conduck !

FIRST B. (*in a superior manner*). Oh, yes ; you soon get into the accent.

> [*Later*—M. CHARLEMAGNE *has re-appeared, and sung a song about changing his apartments, with spoken passages of a pronouncedly Parisian character.*

FIRST B. (*who little suspects what he has been roaring with laughter at*). That fellow really *is* amusing. I must take Nellie to hear him some night before we go back.

SECOND B. (*dubiously*). But aren't some of the songs—for a girl of her age—eh ?

FIRST B. My dear fellow, not a bit ! I give you my word I haven't heard a single line yet that was in the least offensive—not a single line !

*An*ybody might go! Look here—it's Pôlusse next; now you listen—*he'll* make you laugh!

> [*The great* M. PAULUS *appears and sings several Chansons in a confidentially lugubrious tone, and with his forefingers thrust into his waistcoat pockets. Curiously enough, our* FIRST BRITON *is less successful in following* M. PAULUS *than he was with the Artistes who preceded him—but this is entirely owing to the big drum and cymbals, which will keep coming in and putting him out—something in this manner :—*

M. PAULUS. Et quand j'rentr', ce n'est pour rien—
   Ma belle me dit : "Mon pauv' bonhomme,
Tu n'a pas l'air de"—(*The cymbals :* brim-brin-brien!)
Ell' m' flanqu' des giffl's—(*The drum :* pom-pom-pom-pom!)

Refrain (which both Britons understood).

   "Sur le bi—sur le bô ; sur le bô, de bi, de bô.
Sur le bô—sur le bi ; sur le bi, de bô, de bi!" &c., &c., &c.

FIRST BRITON (*after twenty minutes of this sort of thing*). That's the end, I suppose. They've let down the curtain. *Capital*, wasn't he? I could listen to him all night!

SECOND B. (*as they pass out*). So could I—delightful! Don't know when I've enjoyed anything so much. The other people don't seem to be moving, though. (*Consults programme.*) There's another Part after this; Paulus is singing again. I suppose you'll stay?

FIRST B. Well—it's rather late, isn't it?

SECOND B. (*much relieved*). Yes. Not worth while going back now (*with a yawn*). We must come here again.

FIRST B. (*making a mental resolution to return no more*). Oh, we must; nothing like it on our side of the Channel, y' know.

SECOND B. (*with secret gratitude*). No, we can't do it. (*Walk back to their hotel in a state of great mental exhaustion, and finish the evening with a bock on the Boulevards.*)

At a Garden Party.

SCENE—*A London Lawn. A Band in a costume half-way between the uniforms of a stage hussar and a circus groom, is performing under a tree. Guests discovered slowly pacing the turf, or standing and sitting about in groups.*

MRS. MAYNARD GERY (*to her* BROTHER-IN-LAW—*who is thoroughly aware of her little weaknesses*). Oh, Phil,—you know everybody—*do* tell me ! Who is that common-looking little man with the scrubby beard, and the very yellow gloves—how does he come to be *here ?*

PHIL. Where ? Oh, I see him. Well—have you read *Sabrina's Uncle's Other Niece ?*

MRS. M. G. No—*ought* I to have ? I never even heard of it !

PHIL. Really ? I wonder at that—tremendous hit—you must order it—though I doubt if you'll be able to get it.

MRS. M. G. Oh, I shall *insist* on having it. And *he* wrote it ? Really, Phil, now I come to look at him, there's something rather striking about his face. Did you say *Sabrina's Niece's Other Aunt*—or what ?

PHIL. *Sabrina's Uncle's Other Niece* was what I *said*—not that it signifies.

MRS. M. G. Oh, but I always attach the greatest importance to names, myself. And do you know him ?

PHIL. What, Tablett ? Oh, yes—decent little chap ; not much to say for himself, you know.

MRS. M. G. I don't mind *that* when a man is *clever*—do you think you could bring him up and introduce him ?

PHIL. Oh, I *could*—but I won't answer for your not being disappointed in him.

MRS. M. G. I have never been disappointed in any genius *yet*—perhaps, because I don't expect too much—so go, dear boy ; he may be surrounded unless you get hold of him soon.   [Phil *obeys*.

PHIL (*accosting the Scrubby Man*). Well, Tablett, old fellow, how are things going with you ?   *Sabrina* flourishing ?

MR. TABLETT (*enthusiastically*). It's a tremendous hit, my boy ; orders coming in so fast they don't know how to execute 'em—there's a fortune in it, as I always told you !

PHIL. Capital !—but you've such luck.   By the way, my sister-in-law is most anxious to know you.

Mr. T. (*flattered*). Very kind of her. I shall be delighted. I was just thinking I felt quite a stranger here.

PHIL. Come along then, and I'll introduce you. If she asks you to her parties by any chance, mind you go—sure to meet a lot of interesting people.

Mr. T. (*pulling up his collar*). Just what I enjoy—meeting interesting people—the only society worth cultivating, to my mind, Sir. Give me *intellect*—it's of more value than wealth !

[*They go in search of* Mrs. M. G.

FIRST LADY ON CHAIR. Look at the dear Vicar getting that poor Lady Pawperse an ice. What a very spiritual expression he has, to be sure—really quite apostolic !

SECOND LADY. We are not in his parish, but I have always heard him spoken of as a most excellent man.

FIRST LADY. Excellent ! My dear, that man is a perfect *Saint !* I don't believe he knows what it is to have a single worldly thought ! And such trials as he has to bear, too ! With that *dreadful* wife of his !

SECOND LADY. That's the wife, isn't it ?—the dowdy little woman, all alone, over there ?   Dear me, what *could* he have married her for ?

FIRST LADY. Oh, for her *money* of course, my dear !

MRS. PATTALLON (*to* MRS. ST. MARTIN SOMERVILLE). Why, it really *is* you ! I absolutely didn't know you at first. I was just thinking

"Now who *is* that young and lovely person coming along the path?" You see—I came out without my glasses to-day, which accounts for it!

MR. CHUCK (*meeting a youthful Matron and Child*). Ah, Mrs. Sharpe, how de do! *I'm* all right. Hullo, TOTO, how are *you*, eh, young lady?

TOTO (*primly*). I'm very well indeed, thank you. (*With sudden interest.*) How's the idiot? Have you seen him lately?

MR. C. (*mystified*). The idiot, eh? Why, fact is, I don't *know* any idiot!—give you my word!

TOTO (*impatiently*). Yes, you *do—you* know. The one Mummy says you're next door to—you must see him *sometimes!* You *did* say Mr. Chuck was next door to an idiot, didn't you, Mummy? [*Tableau.*

MRS. PRATTLETON. Let me see—*did* we have a fine Summer in '87? Yes, of course—I always remember the weather by the clothes we wore, and that June and July we wore scarcely anything—some filmy stuff that belonged to one's ancestress, don't you know. *Such* fun! By the way, what has become of Lucy?

MRS. ST. PATTICKER. Oh, I've quite lost sight of her lately—you see she's so perfectly happy now, that she's ceased to be in the least interesting!

MRS. HUSSIFFE (*to* MR. DE MURE). Perhaps *you* can tell me of a good coal merchant? The people who supply me now are perfect *fiends*, and I really must go somewhere else.

MR. DE MURE. Then I'm afraid you must be rather difficult to please.

MR. TABLETT *has been introduced to* MRS MAYNARD GERY—*with the following result.*

MRS. M. G. (*enthusiastically*). I'm so delighted to make your acquaintance. When my brother-in-law told me who you were, I positively very nearly shrieked. I am such an admirer of your—(*thinks she won't commit herself to the whole title—and so compounds*)—your delightful *Sabrina!*

MR. T. Most gratified to hear it, I'm sure. I'm told there's a growing demand for it.

MRS. M. G. Such a hopeful sign—when one was beginning quite to despair of the public taste !

MR. T. Well, I've always said—So long as you give the Public a really first-rate article, and are prepared to spend any amount of money on *pushing* it, you know, you're sure to see a handsome return for your outlay —in the long run. And of course you must get it carefully analysed by competent judges—

MRS. M. G. Ah, but *you* can feel independent of criticism now, can't you ?

MR. T. Oh, I defy any one to find anything unwholesome in it—it's as suitable for the most delicate child as it is for adults—nothing to irritate the most sensitive—

MRS. M. G. Ah, you mean certain critics are so thin-skinned—they are indeed !

MR. T. (*warming to his subject*). But the beauty of this particular composition is that it causes absolutely *no* unpleasantness or inconvenience afterwards. In some cases, indeed, it acts like a charm. I've known of two cases of long-standing erysipelas it has completely cured.

MRS. M. G. (*rather at sea*). How gratifying that must be. But that is the magic of all truly great work, it is such an *anodyne*—it takes people so completely out of themselves—doesn't it ?

MR. T. It takes anything of that sort out of *them*, Ma'am. It's the finest discovery of the age, no household will be without it in a few months —though perhaps I say it who shouldn't .

MRS. M. G. (*still more astonished*). Oh, but I *like* to hear you. I'm so tired of hearing people pretending to disparage what they have done, it's such a *pose*, and I hate posing. Real genius is *never* modest. (*If he had been more retiring, she would have, of course, reversed this axiom.*) I *wish* you would come and see me on one of my Tuesdays, MR. TABLETT, I should feel so honoured, and I think you would meet some congenial spirits—do look in some evening—I will send you a card if I may—let me see—could you come and lunch next Sunday ? I've got a little man coming who was very nearly eaten up by cannibals. I think *he* would interest you.

MR. T. I shall be proud to meet him. Er—did they eat *much* of him ?

Mrs. M. G. (*who privately thinks this rather vulgar*). How *witty* you are! That's quite worthy of—er—*Sabrina*, really! Then you *will* come? So glad. And now I mustn't keep you from your other admirers any longer.   [*She dismisses him.*

LATER.

Mrs. M. G. (*to her* Brother-in-law). How *could* you say that dear Mr. Tablett was *dull*, Phil? I found him perfectly charming—so original and unconventional! He's promised to come to me. By the way, *what* did you say the name of his book was?

Phil. *I* never said he had written a book.

Mrs. M. G. Phil—you *did!*—*Sabrina's Other—Something*. Why, I've been *praising* it to him, entirely on your recommendation.

Phil. No, no—*your* mistake. I only asked you if you'd read *Sabrina's Uncle's Other Niece*, and, as I made up the title on the spur of the moment, I should have been rather surprised if you had. *He* never wrote a line in his life.

Mrs. M. G. How *abominable* of you! But surely he's famous for *something?* He talks like it.   [*With reviving hope.*

Phil. Oh, yes, he's the inventor and patentee of the new "Sabrina" Soap—he says he'll make a fortune over it.

Mrs. M. G. But he hasn't even done *that* yet! Phil, I'll *never* forgive you for letting me make such an idiot of myself. What *am* I to do now? I *can't* have him coming to me—he's really too impossible!

Phil. Do? Oh, order some of the soap, and wash your hands of him, I suppose—not that he isn't a good deal more presentable than some of your lions, after all's said and done!

[Mrs. M. G., *before she takes her leave, contrives to inform* Mr. Tablett, *with her prettiest penitence, that she has only just recollected that her luncheon party is put off, and that her Tuesdays are over for the Season. Directly she returns to Town, she promises to let him hear from her; in the meantime, he is not to think of troubling himself to call. So there is no harm done, after all.*

At the Military Tournament.

STENTORIAN JUDGE (*in Arena*). Corporal Binks! (*The Assistants give a finishing blow to the peg, and fall back. Corporal* BINKS *gallops in, misses the peg, and rides off, relieving his feelings by whirling his lance defiantly in the air.*) Corporal Binks—nothing!

A GUSHING LADY. Poor dear thing! I *do* wish he'd struck it! He did look so disappointed, and so did that sweet horse!

THE JUDGE. Sergeant Spanker! (*Sergeant S. gallops in, spears the peg neatly, and carries it off triumphantly on the point of the lance, after which he rides back and returns the peg to the Assistants as a piece of valuable property of which he has accidentally deprived them.*) Sergeant Spanker—eight! (*Applause; the Assistants drive in another peg.*) Corporal Cutlash! (Corporal C. *enters, strikes the peg, and dislodges without securing it. Immense applause from the Crowd.*) Corporal Cutlash—two!

THE GUSHING LADY. Only two, and when he really did hit the peg! I do call that a shame. I should have given him more marks than the other man—he has such a *much* nicer face!

A CHILD WITH A THIRST FOR INFORMATION. Uncle, why do they call it *tent*-pegging?

THE UNCLE. Why? Well, because those pegs are what they fasten down tents with.

THE CHILD. But why isn't there a tent now?

UNCLE. Because there's no use for one.

CHILD. Why?

UNCLE. Because all they want to do is to pick up the peg with the point of their lance.

CHILD. Yes, but why *should* they want to do it?

UNCLE. Oh, to amuse their horses. (*The* CHILD *ponders upon this answer with a view to a fresh catechism upon the equine passion for entertainment, and the desirability, or otherwise, of gratifying it.*)

A CHATTY MAN IN THE PROMENADE (*to his* NEIGHBOUR). Takes a deal of practice to strike them pegs fair and full.

HIS NEIGHBOUR (*who holds advanced Socialistic opinions*). Ah, I dessay—and a pity they can't make no better use o' their time! Spoiling good wood, *I* call it. I don't see no point in it myself.

THE CHATTY MAN. Well, it shows they can *ride*, at any rate.

THE SOCIALIST. Ride? O' course they can *ride*—we pay enough for 'aving 'em taught, don't we? But you mark my words, the People won't put up with this state of things much longer—keepin' a set of 'ired murderers in luxury and hidleness. I tell yer, wherever I come across one of these great lanky louts strutting about in his red coat, as if he was one of the lords of the hearth, well—it makes my nose bleed, ah—it *does!*

THE CHATTY MAN. If that's the way you talk to him, I ain't surprised if it do.

THE JUDGE. Sword *versus* Sword! Come in there! (*Two mounted Combatants, in leather jerkins and black visors, armed with swordsticks, enter the ring;* JUDGE *introduces them to audience with the aid of a flag.*) Corporal JONES, of the Wessex Yeomanry; Sergeant SMITH, of the Manx Mounted Infantry. (*Their swords are chalked by the Assistants.*) Are you ready? Left turn! Countermarch! Engage! (*The Combatants wheel round and face one another, each vigorously spurring his horse and prodding cautiously at the other; the two horses seem determined not to be drawn into the affair themselves on any account, and take no personal interest in the conflict; the umpires skip and dodge at the rear of the horses, until one of the Combatants gets in with a rattling blow on the other's head, to the intense delight of audience. Both men are brushed down, and their weapons re-chalked, whereupon they engage once more—much to the disgust of their horses, who had evidently been hoping it was all over. After the contest is finally decided, a second pair of Combatants enter; one is mounted on a black horse, the other on a chestnut, who refuses to lend himself to the business on any terms, and bolts on principle; while the rider of the black horse remains in stationary meditation.)* Go on—that black horse—go on! (*The chestnut is at length brought up to the scratch snorting, but again flinches, and retires with his rider.*)

THE CROWD (*to rider of black horse*). Go on, now's your chance! 'It him! (*The recipient of these counsels pursues his antagonist, and belabours him and his horse with impartial good-will until separated by the Umpires, who examine the chalk-marks with a professional scrutiny.*)

THE JUDGE. Here, you on the black horse, you mustn't hit that other horse about the head. (*The man addressed appears rebuked and surprised under his black-wired visor.*) The JUDGE (*reassuringly*). It's all *right*, you know; only, don't do it again, that's all! (*The Combatant sits up again.*)

THE GUSHING LADY. Oh, I can't bear to look on, really. I'm *sure* they oughtn't to hit so hard—*how* their poor dear heads must ache! Isn't that chestnut a *duck*? I'm sure he's trying to save his master from getting hurt—they're such sensible creatures, horses are! (*Artillery teams drive in, and gallop between the posts; the Crowd going frantic with delight when the posts remain upright, and roaring with laughter when one is knocked over.*)

DURING THE MUSICAL RIDE.

THE GUSHING LADY. Oh, they're simply too *sweet!* How those horses are enjoying it—aren't they pets? and how perfectly they keep step to the music, don't they?

HER FRIEND. (*who is beginning to get a trifle tired by her enthusiasm*). Yes; but then they're all trained by Madame Katti Lanner, of Drury Lane, you see.

THE GUSHING LADY. What pains she must have taken with them; but you can teach a horse *anything*, can't you?

HER FRIEND. Oh, that's nothing; next year they're going to have a horse who'll dance the Highland Fling.

THE SOCIALIST. A pretty sight? Cost a pretty sight o' the People's money, I know that. Tomfoolery, that's what it is; a set of dressed-up bullies dancin' quadrilles on 'orseback; *that* ain't military manœuvrin'. It's sickenin' the way fools applaud such goin's on. And cuttin' off the Saracen's 'ed, too; I'd call it plucky if the Saracen 'ad a gun in his 'and. Bah, I 'ate the 'ole business!

HIS NEIGHBOUR. Got anybody along with you, Mate?

THE SOCIALIST. No, I don't want anybody along with *me*, I don't.

HIS NEIGHBOUR. That's a pity, that is. A sweet-tempered, pleasant-spoken party like you are oughtn't to go about by yourself. You ought to bring somebody just to enjoy your conversation. There don't seem to be anybody '*cre* of your way of thinkin'.

DURING THE COMBINED DISPLAY.

THE GUSHING LADY (*as the Cyclist Corps enter*). Oh, they've got a *dog* with them. Do look—such a dear! See, they've tied a letter round his neck. He'll come back with an answer presently. (*But, there being apparently no answer to this communication, the faithful but prudent animal does not re-appear.*)

AFTER THE PERFORMANCE.

THE INQUISITIVE CHILD. Uncle, which side won?

UNCLE. I suppose the side that advanced across the bridges.

CHILD. Which side *would* have won if it had been a *real* battle?

UNCLE. I really couldn't undertake to say, my boy.

CHILD. But which do you *think* would have won?

UNCLE. I suppose the side that fought best.

CHILD. But which side was *that?* (*The* Uncle *begins to find that the society of an intelligent* Nephew *entails too severe a mental strain to be frequently cultivated.*)

Free Speech.

SCENE—*An Open Space. Rain falling in torrents. An Indignation Meeting is being held to protest against the Royal Grants. The Chairman presides at a small portable reading-desk, generally alluded to as The " Nostrum" ; a ring of more or less Earnest Radicals, under umbrellas, surround him. Speakers address the Meeting in rapid succession; a Man with a red flag gives it a sinister wave at any particularly vigorous expression. Her Gracious Majesty the Queen is repeatedly described as " this mis-rubble ole bein' ," an Archbishop is invariably mentioned as an " Arch-rogue," while the orators and the audience appear from their remarks to be the only persons capable of worthily guiding this unhappy Country's destinies. Policemen in couples look on from a distance and smile indulgently.*

AN ORATOR (*bitterly*). The weather is against us, Feller Republi-kins, there's no denyin' that.   As we were tramping along 'ere, through the mud and in the rain, wet to the skin, I couldn't 'elp remarking to a friend o' mine, that if it had been a pidging-shootin' match at Urlingham, or a Race-meeting at Hascot, things 'ud ha' been diff'rent ! Ther'd ha' bin blue sky and sunshine enough *then*. Well, I 'spose hany weather's con-sidered good enongh for the likes of hus ! Hany weather 'll do for pore downtrod slaves to assert their man'ood and their hindependence in ! (*Cries of " Shame !"*) Never you mind—hour turn 'll come some day ! We sha'n't *halways* be 'eld down, and muzzled, and silenced, and prevented uttering the hindignation we've a right to feel ! (*Bellowing.*) We shall make our vices 'eard one day ! But I'm reminded by my friend as I've got to keep to the pint.   Well (*he composes his features into a sneer*) I'm

told as 'ow 'Er Most Gracious Madjesty—(" *Booing" from Earnest Radicals*)
—'Er Most Gracious Madjesty—'as she calls 'erself—'as put by a little
matter of a millum an' a 'arf—since she came to the Throne. Now, Feller
Republikins, that millum an' a 'arf 'as come out of *your* pockets !

SEVERAL PERSONS (*who do not* look *as if they paid a heavy income
tax*). 'Ear 'ear !

ORATOR. Yes, it belongs to the People—ah! and you've a legal right
to demand it back—a legal *right !* And I arsk you—if that millum and a
'arf of money was to be divided among the Toilers of London ter-morrow
—'ow many Hunemployed should we see ? (*Crowd deeply impressed by
this forcible argument.*) Yet we're arst to put our 'ands in our pockets to
support the Queen's children !

A GENTLEMAN WITH VERY SHORT HAIR. Shame—never ! [*Puts his
hand in somebody else's pocket by way of emphasising his declaration.*]

ORATOR. Feller Republikins, if a Queen don't do the work as she's
paid for doin' of, what ought to be done with 'er ? I put it to *you !*

A VERY EARNEST RADICAL. The Scaffild !

[*Looks round nervously to see if a Policeman is within hearing.*

A FAT LADY (*who has been ejaculating.* "Oh, it is a shime, it is !"
at every fresh instance of Royal expenditure). Well, I must say that's
rather strong langwidge !

ANOTHER ORATOR. Gentlemen, I regret to say that, on this mon-
strous fraud and attempted imposition known as "The Royal Grants
Bill," Mr. Gladstone voted with the Government.   [*Frantic applause.*

ORATOR (*puzzled*). Yes, Gentlemen, I am here to state facts, and I
am ashamed to say, that on this single occasion Mr. Gladstone—went
wrong.   [*Shouts of "No! No!"*

A FERVID GLADSTONIAN (*waving his umbrella*). Three cheers for
Mr. Gladstone, what-*hever* he does !

[*The* CROWD *join in heartily;* ORATOR *decides to drop the point, particularly as it does not seem to affect the Meeting's condemnation of
the principle of the Bill.*

AN IRISH PATRIOT. I've often harrd tell, Gintlemen, of a certain
stra-ange animal they carl a "Conservative Warkin-Man" (*Roars of*

laughter). A Warkin-Man a Conservative! Why, bliss me sowl, the thing's absurd! There niver *was* such a purrson in this Warld. A Conservative Warkin-Man! why—(*takes refuge in profanity*). If there was why don't we iver hear 'um in an assimbly of this sort? Why hasn't he the common manly courage to come forward and defind his opinions? *We'd* hear 'um, Gintlemen. It's the proud boast of Radicals and Republikins that they'd give free speech and a fair hearin' to ivery man, no matter hwhat his opinions are, but ye'll niver see 'um stip farward at ahl—and hwhy?

A DECENT MECHANIC. Well, look 'ere, mate, *I'm* a Conservative Working-Man, if ye'd like to know, and I ain't afraid to defend my opinions. Come now!

THE CHAIRMAN (*somewhat taken aback*). Well, Friends, while I conduct this chair, I can promise this man a puffickly fair 'earin', and I'm sure you will listen to him patiently, whatever you may think of his arguments. (*Cries of 'Ear—'ear!* "*Fair play hall the world hover!*" "*We'll listen to him quiet enough!*") First of all, I must be satisfied that our Friend is what he professes to be. We want no Sham Workin'-men 'ere. [*Brandishes a foot-rule in evidence of the genuineness of his own claims.*

THE D. M. Am I a workin'-man? Well, I've made ladies' boots at sixpence an hour for three years—d'ye call that bein' a Workin' Man? I've soled and 'eeled while you wait in a stall near Southwark Bridge seven years an' a arf! Praps you'll call *that* a Workin'-Man? (*Cries of "Keep to the Point!*") Oh, I'll keep to the point right enough. There's this Irishman here been a tellin' of you 'ow wrong it is to turn his countrymen out of their 'ouses when they don't pay their rent. Ain't *we* turned out of our 'ouses, if we don't pay ourn? 'Oo snivels over *hus?*

THE I. P. No personalities now! It's my belief ye're a Landlord yerself! [*Uproar.*

THE D. M. I *told* yer ye wouldn't 'ear me now!

A SOCIALIST (*in a stentorian voice*). Feller Demmercrats, as an ex-Fenian and an ex-Convict, I implore you—give this man a hearin'!

THE D. M. Then about this Royal Grant. (*Cries of "Shut up!*" "*Go 'ome!*" "*Don't tork nonsense!*") If you're going to 'ave a King and

"SHOW IT NOW, BY PUTTING MONEY IN THIS 'AT!"

Queen at all—(*Cries of* "*We ain't! Down with 'em !*") Ah, then I s'pose you're going to put up fellers like 'im (*pointing to the Socialist*), and 'im (*pointing to Chairman*), and 'im ! [*Uproar.*

THE SOCIALIST. Fellow-Citizens, I appeal to you, give this man rope —he's doing our work splendidly !

THE D. M. Well, all I've got to say is——(*Shouts of* "*Get down !*" *Yells and booing*). Oh, you won't tire me out that way. All *I* can say is, I'd a precious sight rather——

THE CHAIRMAN (*excitedly*). Fellow citizens, we've listened to this man long enough—these sentiments are an insult to the meeting !
[*Yells as before.*

THE SOCIALIST (*extending a billycock hat with a passionate gesture*). Feller Demmercrats, if you are earnest, if you are sincere in the indigna-tion, the just hindignation, this man provokes—show it now, by putting money in this 'at for the Plan o' Campaign ! [*The storm lulls.*

THE D. M. (*resuming*). I arsk every honest man here whether—— *Chairman* (*interposing*). I think, as our friend here don't seem able to keep to his point, we won't call upon him for any further remarks.

[THE D. M. *is hustled down, amidst derisive cheers and groans ; the* SOCIALIST *ascends the Platform.*

THE SOCIALIST. I don't mind tellin' yer, friends and feller citizens, that in the late election in Heast Marylebone, I used all my influence— (*cheers*)—all *my* influence to deter men from voting for your Radical candidate. (*Sensation, and a cry of* "*More shame for yer !*") Ah, I *did*, though, and I'd do it agin, and I'll tell yer for why. I 'ate yer Tories, but if I'm to be 'it a blow in the face, I don't like it done behind my back. (*Cheers*). And your precious Liberals and. Radicals, they're worse nor hany Tories, and for this reason—(*with a penetrating glance*)—they're more hinvidious ! Ah, that's it, they're more *hinvidious !* Traitors, hevery man jack of 'em !

[*And so on, concluding with denunciations of all* "*sending round the 'at,*" *and appeals for contributions to the Plan of Campaign. Meeting dissolves with three cheers for the coming Republic from the victims of a Tyrannous System of Repression of Opinion.*

The Riding-Class.

SCENE—*A Riding-school, on a raw chilly afternoon. The gas is lighted, but does not lend much cheerfulness to the interior, which is bare and bleak, and pervaded by a bluish haze. Members of the Class discovered standing about on the tan, waiting for their horses to be brought in. At the further end is an alcove, with a small balcony, in which* MRS. BILBOW-KAY, *the Mother of one of the Equestrians, is seated with a young female Friend.*

MRS. BILBOW-KAY. Oh, Robert used to ride very nicely indeed when he was a boy ; but he has been out of practice lately, and so, as the Doctor ordered him horse-exercise, I thought it would be wiser for him to take a few lessons. Such an excellent change for any one with sedentary pursuits !

THE FRIEND. But isn't riding a sedentary pursuit, too ?

MRS. B.·K. Robert says *he* doesn't find it so.

[*Enter the* RIDING MASTER.

RIDING MASTER (*saluting with cane*). Evenin', Gentlemen—your 'orses will be in directly ; 'ope we shall see some *ridin'* this time. (*Clatter without ; enter Stablemen with horses.*) Let me see—Mr. Bilbow-Kay, Sir, you'd better ride the *Shar ;* he ain't been out all day, so he'll want some 'andling. (Mr. B.-K., *with a sickly smile, accepts a tall and lively horse.*) No, Mr. Tongs, that ain't *your* 'orse to-day—you've got beyond 'im, Sir. We'll put you up on *Lady Loo ;* she's a bit rough till you get on terms with her, but you'll be all right on her after a bit. Yes, Mr. Joggles, Sir, you take *Kangaroo*, please. Mr. Bumpas, I've 'ad the *Artful Dodger* out for you ; and mind he don't get rid of you so easy as he did Mr. Gripper

"YOU AIN'T NO MORE 'OLD ON THAT SADDLE THAN A STAMP WITH THE GUM LICKED OFF!"

last time. Got a nice 'orse for *you*, Mr. 'Arry Sniggers, Sir—*Frar Diavolo*. You mustn't take no notice of his bucking a bit at starting—he'll soon leave it off.

MR. SNIGGERS (*who conceals his qualms under a forced facetiousness*). Soon leave *me* off you mean!

R. M. (*after distributing the remaining horses*). Now then—bring your 'orses up into line, and stand by, ready to mount at the word of command, reins taken up in the left 'and with the second and little fingers, and a lock of the 'orse's mane twisted round the first. Mount! That 'orse ain't a *bicycle*, Mr. Sniggers. [Mr. S. (*in an undertone*). No—worse luck!] Number off! Walk! I shall give the word to trot directly, so now's the time to improve your seats—that back a bit straighter, Mr. 'Ooper. No. 4 just fall out, and we'll let them stirrup-leathers down another 'ole or two for yer. (*No. 4, who has just been congratulating himself that his stirrups were conveniently high, has to see them let down to a distance where he can just touch them by stretching.*) Now you're all comfortable. ["Oh, *are* we?" *from* MR. S.] Trot! Mr. Tongs, Sir, 'old that 'orse in—he's gettin' away with you already. Very bad, Mr. Joggles, Sir—keep those 'eels down! Lost your stirrup, Mr. Jelly? Never mind that—*feel* for it, Sir. I want you to be independent of the irons. I'm going to make you ride without 'em presently. (Mr. Jelly *shivers in his saddle.*) Captin' Cropper, Sir; if that Volunteer ridgment as you're goin' to be the Major of sees you like you are now, on a field-day—they'll 'ave to fall out to *larf*, Sir! (Mr. Cropper *devoutly wishes he had been less ingenuous as to his motive for practising his riding.*) Now, Mr. Sniggers, make that 'orse learn 'oo's the master! [Mr. S. "He *knows*, the brute!"]

MRS. B.-K. He's very rude to all the Class, except dear Robert—but then Robert has such a nice easy seat.

THE R. M. Mr. Bilbow-Kay, Sir, try and set a bit closer. Why, you ain't no more 'old on that saddle than a stamp with the gum licked off! Can-ter! *You're* all right, Mr. Joggles—it's on'y his play; set down on your saddle, Sir! . . . I didn't say on the ground!

MRS. B.-K. (*anxiously to her* SON, *as he passes*). Bob, are you quite sure you're safe? (*To* FRIEND.) His horse is snorting so dreadfully!

R. M. 'Alt! Every Gentleman take his feet out of the stirrups, and cross them on the saddle in front of him. Not your *feet*, Mr. Sniggers, we ain't Turks 'ere!

MR. S. (*sotto voce*). "There's *one* bloomin' Turk 'ere, anyway!"

R. M. Now then—Walk! . . . Trot! Set back, Gentlemen, set back all—'old on by your knees, not the pommels. *I* see you, Mr. Jelly, kitchin' old o' the mane—I shall 'ave to give you a 'ogged 'orse next time you come. Quicken up a bit—this is a ride, not a funeral. Why, I could *roll* faster than you're trotting! Lor, you're like a row o' Guy Foxes on 'orseback, you are! Ah, I thought I'd see one o' you orf! Goa-ron, all o' you, you don't come 'ere to *play* at ridin'—I'll make you ride afore I've done with you! 'Ullo, Mr. Joggles, nearly gone that time, Sir! There, that'll do—or we'll 'ave all your saddles to let unfurnished. Wa—alk! Mr. Bilbow-Kay, when your 'orse changes his pace sudden, it don't look well for you to be found settin' 'arf way up his neck, and it gives him a bad opinion of yer, Sir. Uncross stirrups! Trot on! It ain't no mortal use your clucking to that mare, Mr. Tongs, Sir, because she don't understand the langwidge—touch her with your 'eel in the ribs. Mr. Sniggers, that 'orse is doin' jest what he likes with you. 'It 'im, Sir; he's no friends and few relations!

Mr. S. (*with spirit*). *I* ain't going to 'it 'im. If you want him 'it, get up and do it yourself!

R. M. When I say "Circle Right"—odd numbers'll wheel round and fall in be'ind even ones. Circle *Right!* . . . Well, if ever I—I didn't tell yer to fall *off* be'ind. Ketch your 'orses and stick to 'em next time. Right In-*cline!* O' course, Mr. Joggles, if you prefer takin' that animal for a little ride all by himself we'll let you out in the streets—otherwise p'raps you'll kindly follow yer leader. Captain Cropper, Sir, if you let that curb out a bit more, *Reindeer* wouldn't be 'arf so narsty with yer. . . Ah, now you 'ave done it. You want *your* reins painted different colours and labelled, Sir, you do. 'Alt, the rest of you. . . Now, seein' you're shook down in your saddles a bit—[" *Shook up's more like it!*" *from* Mr. S.]—we'll 'ave the 'urdles in and show you a bit o' Donnybrook! (*The Class endeavours to assume an air of delighted anticipation at this pleasing prospect.*) *To* Assistant R. M., *who has entered and said something in an undertone.*) Eh,

Captin' ' Edstall here, and wants to try the grey cob over 'urdles? Ask him if he'll come in now—we're just going to do some jumping.

ASSIST. R. M. This lot don't look much like going over 'urdles—'cept in front o' the 'orse, but I'll tell the Captain.

[*The hurdles are brought in and propped up. Enter a well-turned-out* STRANGER, *on a grey cob.*

MR. SNIGGERS (*to him*). You ain't lost nothing by coming late, I can tell yer. We've bin having a gay old time in 'ere—made us ride without sterrups, he did!

CAPTAIN HEADSTALL. Haw, really? Didn't get grassed, did you?

MR. S. Well, me and my 'orse separated by mutual consent. I ain't what you call a fancy 'orseman. We've got to go at that 'urdle in a minute. How do *you* like the ideer, eh? It's no good funking it—it's got to be *done!*

R. M. Now, Captin—not *you*, Captin Cropper—Captin 'Edstall *I* mean, will you show them the way over, please?

[CAPTAIN H. *rides at it; the cob jumps too short, and knocks the hurdle down—to his rider's intense disgust.*

MR. S. I say, Guvnor, that was a near thing. I wonder you weren't off.

CAPT. H. I—ah—don't often come off.

MR. S. You won't say that when you've been 'ere a few times. You see, they've put you on a quiet animal this journey. *I* shall try to get him myself next time. He be'aves like a gentleman, *he* does.

CAPT. H. You won't mount him, if you take my advice—he has rather a delicate mouth.

MR. S. Oh, I don't mind that—I should ride him on the curb o' course.

[*The Class ride at the hurdle one by one.*

R. M. Now, Mr. Sniggers, give 'im more of 'is 'ed than that, Sir—or he'll take it . . . Oh, Lor, well, it's soft falling luckily! Mr. Joggles, Sir, keep him back till you're in a line with it . . . Better, Sir; you come down true on your saddle afterwards anyway! . . . Mr. Parabole! . . . Ah, *would* you? *Told* you he was tricky, Sir! Try him at it again . . . Now—over! . . . Yes, and it is over, and no mistake!

MRS B.-K. Now it's Robert's turn. I'm afraid he's been overtiring himself, he looks so pale. Bob, you won't let him jump too high, *will* you? —Oh, I daren't look. Tell me, my love,—is he *safe?*

HER FRIEND. Perfectly—they're just brushing him down.

AFTERWARDS.

MRS. B.-K. (*to her* SON). Oh, Bob, you must never think of jumping again—it *is* such a dangerous amusement!

ROBERT (*who has been cursing the hour in which he informed his parent of the exact whereabouts of the school*). It's all right with a horse that knows *how* to jump. Mine didn't.

THE FRIEND. I *thought* you seemed to jump a good deal higher than the horse did. They ought to be trained to keep close under you, oughtn't they? [ROBERT *wonders if she is as guileless as she looks.*]

CAPT. CROPPER (*to the* R. M.) Oh, takes about eight months, with a lesson every day, to make a man efficient in the Cavalry, does it? But, look here—I suppose four more lessons will put *me* all right, eh? I've had *eight*, y' know.

R. M. Well, Sir, if you *arsk* me, I dunno as another arf dozen 'll do you any 'arm—but, o'course, that's just as *you* feel about it.

[CAPTAIN CROPPER *endeavours to extract encouragement from this Delphic response.*]

The Impromptu Charade-Party.

SCENE—*The Library of a Country-House ; the tables and chairs are heaped with brocades, draperies, and properties of all kinds, which the Ladies of the company are trying on, while the men rack their brains for a suitable Word. In a secluded corner,* MR. NIGHTINGALE *and* MISS ROSE *are conversing in whispers.*

MR. WHIPSTER (*Stage-Manager and Organizer—self-appointed*). No—but I say, *really*, you know, we *must* try and decide on something—we've been out half-an-hour, and the people will be getting impatient! (*To the Ladies.*) Do come and help; it's really no use dressing up till we've settled what we're going *to do.* Can't *anybody* think of a good Word?

MISS LARKSPUR. We ought to make a continuous story of it, with the same plot and characters all through. We did that once at the Grange, and it was awfully good—just like a regular Comedy!

MR. WHIPSTER. Ah, but we've got to hit on *a Word* first. Come—nobody got an idea? Nightingale, you're not much use over *there*, you know. I hope you and Miss Rose have been putting your heads together?

MR. NIGHTINGALE (*confused*). Eh? No, nothing of the sort! Oh, ah—yes, we've thought of a *lot* of Words.

MISS ROSE. Only you've driven them all out of our heads again!

[*They resume their conversation.*

MR. WHI. Well, do make a suggestion, somebody! Professor, won't *you* give us a Word?

CHORUS OF LADIES. Oh, *do*, Professor—you're sure to think of something clever!

PROFESSOR POLLEN (*modestly*).　Well, really, I've so little experience in these matters that—A Word *has* just occurred to me, however ; I don't know, of course, whether it will meet with approval—(*he beams at them with modest pride through his spectacles*)—it's " Monocotyledonous."

CHORUS OF LADIES.　Charming !　Monocottle—Oh, can't we *do* that ?

MR. WH. (*dubiously*).　We might—but —cr—what's it *mean ?*

PROF. POLLEN.　It's a simple botanical term, signifying a plant which has only one cup-shaped leaf, or seed-lobe.　Plants with *two* are termed—

MR. WH.　I don't see how we're going to act a plant with only one seed-lobe myself—and then the syllables—" mon "—" oh "—" cot "—" till " —we shouldn't get done before *midnight*, you know !

PROF. POLLEN (*with mild pique*).　Well, I merely threw it out as a suggestion.　I thought it could have been made amusing.　No doubt I was wrong ; no doubt.

MR. SETTEE (*nervously*).　I've thought of a word.　How would—er— " *Familiar* " do

MR. WH. (*severely*).　Now, *really*, Settee, *do* try not to footle like this !
　　　　　　　　　　[MR. SETTEE *subsides amidst general disapproval.*

MR. FLINDERS (*with a flash of genius*).　I've got it—*Gamboge !*

MR. WH.　Gamboge, eh ?　Let's see how that would work :—" Gam "- " booge."　How do you see it yourself ?

　　　　　[MR. FLINDERS *discovers on reflection, that he doesn't see it, and the suggestion is allowed to drop.*

MISS PELAGIA RHYS.　*I've* an idea.　*Familiar !*　" Fame "-" ill "-" liar," you know.　　　　　　　　　　　　　　[*Chorus of applause.*

MR. WH.　Capital !　The very thing—congratulate you, Miss Rhys !

MR. SETTEE (*sotto voce*).　But I say, look here, *I* suggested that, you know, and you said— !

MR. WH. (*ditto*).　What on earth *does* it matter who suggests it, so long as it's right ?　Don't be an ass, Settee !　(*Aloud.*)　How are we going to do the first syllable " Fame," eh ?　　　　　　　[MR. SETTEE *sulks.*

MR. PUSHINGTON.　Oh, that's easy.　One of us must come on as a Poet, and all the ladies must crowd round flattering him, and making a lot

of him, asking him for his autograph, and so on.   I don't mind doing the
Poet myself, if nobody else feels up to it.

> [*He begins to dress for the part by turning his dress-coat inside out,
> and putting on a turban and a Liberty sash, by way of indi-
> cating the eccentricity of genius ; the Ladies adorn themselves
> with a similar regard to realism, and even more care for
> appearances.*

AFTER THE FIRST SYLLABLE.

The Performers return from the drawing-room, followed by faint applause.

MR. PUSHINGTON.   Went capitally, that syllable, eh ?   (*No response.*)
You might have played up to me a little more than you did—you others.
You let me do everything !

MISS LARKSPUR.   You never let any of us get a word in !

MR. PUSHINGTON.   Because you all talked at once, that was all.   Now
then—"ill."   I'll be a celebrated Doctor, and you all come to me one by
one, and say you're *ill*—see ?

> [*Attires himself for the rôle of a Physician in a dressing-gown and
> an old yeomanry helmet.*

MR. WHIPSTER (*huffily*).   Seems to me I may as well go and sit with
the audience—I'm no use *here !*

MR. PUSHINGTON.   Oh, yes, Whipster, I want you to be my
confidential butler, and show the patients in.

> [MR. W. *accepts—with a view to showing* PUSHINGTON *that other
> people can act as well as he.*

AFTER THE SECOND SYLLABLE.

MR. PUSHINGTON.   Seemed to *drag* a little, somehow !   There was no
necessity for you to make all those long soliloquies, Whipster.   A Doctor's
confidential servant wouldn't chatter so much !

MR. WHIPSTER.   You were so confoundedly solemn over it, I had to
put some fun in *somewhere !*

MR. P.   Well, you might have put it where some one could see it.
Nobody laughed.

PROFESSOR POLLEN. I don't know, Mr. Pushington, why, when I was describing my symptoms—which I can vouch for as scientifically correct—you persisted in kicking my legs under the table—it was unprofessional, Sir, and extremely painful!

MR. PUSHINGTON. I was only trying to hint to you that as there were a dozen other people to follow, it was time you cut the interview short, Professor—that one syllable alone has taken nearly an hour.

MISS BUCKRAM. If I had known the kind of questions you were going to ask me, Mr. Pushington, I should certainly not have exposed myself to them. I say no more, but I must positively decline to appear with you again.

MR. PUSHINGTON. Oh, but really, you know, in Charades one gets carried away at times. I assure you, I hadn't the remotest (*&c., &c.—until* Miss Buckram *is partly mollified.*) Now then—last syllable. Look here, I'll be a regular impostor, don't you know, and all of you come on and say what a *liar* I am. We ought to make that screamingly funny!

AFTER THE THIRD SYLLABLE.

MR. PUSHINGTON. Muddled? Of *course* it was muddled—you all called me a liar before I opened my mouth!

THE REST. But you didn't seem to know how to begin, and we *had* to bring the Word in somehow.

PUSHINGTON. Bring it in?—but you needn't have let it *out*. There was Settee there, shouting " liar " till he was black in the face. We must have looked a set of idiots from the front. I sha'n't go in again (*muttering*). It's no use acting Charades with people who don't understand it. There ; settle the Word yourselves!

AFTER THE WORD. AMONG THE AUDIENCE.

GENERAL MURMUR. What *can* it be ? Not *Turk*, I suppose, or Magician ?—Quarrelling ?—Parnellite ?—Impertinence ? Shall we give it up? No, they like us to guess, poor things ; and besides, if we don't they'll do another ; and it is getting *so* late, and such a *long* drive home. Oh, they're all coming back; then it *is* over. No, indeed, we can't *imagine.* "*Familiar!*" To be sure—*how* clever, and *how* well you all acted it, to be sure—you must be quite tired after it all. I am sure *we*—hem—are deeply indebted to you. . . . My dear Miss Rose, how wonderfully you disguised yourself, I never recognized you a bit, nor *you*, Mr. Nightingale. What part did *you* take?

MR. NIGHTINGALE. I—er—didn't take any particular part—wasn't wanted, you know.

MISS ROSE. Not to *act*,—so we stayed outside and—and—arranged things.

AN OLD LADY. Indeed? Then you had all the hard work, and none of the pleasure, my dear, I'm afraid.

MISS ROSE (*sweetly*). Oh no. I mean yes!—but we didn't *mind* it much.

THE O. L. And which of you settled what the Word was to be?

MR. N. Well, I believe we settled that together.

> [*Carriages are announced ; departure of guests who are not of the house-party. In the Smoking-room,* MR. PUSHINGTON *discovers that he does not seem exactly popular with the other men, and puts it down to jealousy.*

A Christmas Romp.

SCENE—MRS. CHIPPERFIELD'S *Drawing-room. It is after the Christmas dinner, and the Gentlemen have not yet appeared. MRS. C. is laboriously attempting to be gracious to her Brother's Fiancée, whose acquaintance she has made for the first time, and with whom she is disappointed. Married Sisters and Maiden Aunts confer in corners with a sleepy acidity.*

FIRST MARRIED SISTER (*to Second*). I felt quite sorry for Fred, to see him sitting there, looking—and no wonder—so ashamed of himself—but I always will say, and I always *must* say, Caroline, that if you and Robert had been *firmer* with him when he was younger, he would never have turned out so badly ! Now, there's my George—&c., &c.

MRS. C. (*to the Fiancée*). Well, my dear, I don't approve of young men getting engaged until they have some prospect of being able to marry, and dear Algy was always my favourite brother, and I've seen so much misery from long engagements. However, we must hope for the best, that's all !

A MAIDEN AUNT (*to Second Ditto*). Exactly what struck *me*, Martha. *One* waiter would have been quite sufficient, and if James *must* be grand and give champagne, he might have given us a little *more* of it; I'm sure I'd little else but foam in *my* glass ! And every plate as cold as a stone, and you and I the only people who were not considered worthy of silver forks, and the children encouraged to behave as they please, and Joseph Podmore made such a fuss with, because he's well off—and not enough sweetbread to go the round. Ah, well, thank goodness, we needn't dine here for another year !

MR. CHIPPERFIELD (*at the door*). Sorry to cut you short in your cigar, Uncle, and you, Limpett; but fact is, being Christmas night, I thought we'd come up a little sooner and all have a bit of a romp . . . Well, Emily, my dear, here we are, all of us—ready for anything in the way of a frolic—what's it to be? Forfeits, games, Puss in the Corner, something to cheer us all up, eh? Won't any one make a suggestion?

[*General expression of gloomy blankness.*

ALGERNON (*to his Fiancée—whom he wants to see shine*). Zeffie, you know no end of games—what's that one you played at home, with potatoes and a salt-spoon, *you* know?

ZEFFIE (*blushing*). No, *please*, Algy! I don't know *any* games, indeed, I couldn't *really!*

MR. C. Uncle Joseph will set us going, I'm sure—what do *you* say, Uncle?

UNCLE JOSEPH. Well, I won't say "no" to a quiet rubber.

MRS. C. But, you see, we can't *all* play in that, and there *is* a pack of cards in the house somewhere; but I know two of the aces are gone, and I don't think all the court cards were there the last time we played. Still, if you can manage with what is left, we might get up a game for you.

UNCLE J. (*grimly*). Thank you, my dear, but, on the whole, I think I would almost rather romp—

MR. C. Uncle Joseph votes for romping! What do you say to Dumb Crambo? Great fun—half of us go out, and come in on all-fours, to rhyme to "cat," or "bat," or something—*you* can play that, Limpett?

MR. LIMPETT. If I *must* find a rhyme to cat, I prefer, so soon after dinner, not to go on all-fours for it, I confess.

MR. C. Well, let's have something quieter, then—only *do* settle. Musical Chairs, eh?

ALGY. Zeffie will play the piano for you—she plays beautifully.

ZEFFIE. Not without notes, Algy, and I forgot to bring my music with me. Shall we play "Consequences"? It's a very quiet game—you play it sitting down, with paper and pencil, you know!

MR. LIMPETT (*sardonically, and sotto voce*). Ah, this is something *like* a rollick now. "Consequences," eh?

ALGY (*who has overheard—in a savage undertone*). If that isn't good enough for you, suggest something better—or shut up!

[MR. L. *prefers the latter alternative.*

MR. C. Now, then, have you given everybody a piece of paper, Emily? Caroline, you're going to play—we can't leave *you* out of it.

AUNT CAROLINE. No, James, I'd rather look on, and see you all enjoying yourselves—I've *no* animal spirits now!

MR. C. Oh, nonsense! Christmas-time, you know. Let's be jolly while we can—give her a pencil, Emily!

AUNT C. No, I can't, really. You must excuse me. I know I'm a wet blanket; but, when I think that I mayn't be with you another Christmas, we may *most* of us be dead by then, why—(*sobs*).

FRED (*the Family Failure*). That's right, Mater—trust you to see the humorous side of everything!

ANOTHER AUNT. For shame, Fred! If you don't know who is responsible for your poor mother's low spirits, others do!

[*The Family Failure collapses*

MR. LIMPETT. Well, as we've all got pencils, is there any reason why the revelry should not commence?

MR. C. No—don't let's waste any more time. Miss Zeffie says she will write down on the top of her paper "Who met whom" (must be a Lady and Gentleman in the party, you know), then she folds it down, and passes it on to the next, who writes, "What he said to her"—the next. "What she said to him"—next, "What the consequences were," and the last, "What the world said." Capital game—first-rate. Now, then!

[*The whole party pass papers in silence from one to another, and scribble industriously with knitted brows.*

MR. C. Time's up, all of you. I'll read the first paper aloud. (*Glances at it, and explodes.*) He-he!—this is really very funny. (*Reads.*) "Uncle Joseph met Aunt Caroline at the—ho—ho!—the Empire! He said to her, '*What are the wild waves saying!*' and she said to him, 'It's time you were taken away!' The consequences were that they both went and had their hair cut, and the world said they had always suspected there was something between them!"

UNCLE J.   I consider that a piece of confounded impertinence!

[*Puffs.*

AUNT C.   It's not true.   I *never* met Joseph at the Empire.   I don't go to such places.   I *didn't* think I should be insulted like this—(*Weeps*) —on Christmas too!

AUNTS' CHORUS.   Fred *again!*

[*They regard the* FAMILY FAILURE *indignantly.*

MR. C.   There, there, it was all fun—no harm meant.   I'll read the next.   "Mr. Limpett met Miss Zeffie in the Burlington Arcade.   He said to her, 'O, you little duck!'   She said to him, 'Fowls are cheap to-day!'   The consequences were that they never smiled again, and the world said, 'What price hot potatoes?'"   (*Everybody looks depressed.*)   H'm—not bad—but I think we'll play something else now.

[ZEFFIE *perceives that* ALGY *is not pleased with her.*

TOMMY (*to* UNCLE JOSEPH).   Uncle, why didn't *you* carve at dinner?

UNCLE J.   Well, Tommy, because the carving was done at a side table—and uncommon badly done, too.   Why do you want to know?

TOMMY.   Parpar thought you *would* carve, I know.   He told Mummy she must ask you, because—

MRS. C. (*with a prophetic instinct*).   Now, Tommy, you mustn't tease your Uncle.   Come away, and tell your new Aunt Zeffie what you're going to do with your Christmas boxes.

TOMMY.   But mayn't I tell him what Parpar said, first?

MRS. C.   No, no; by and by—not now!   [*She averts the danger.*

[*Later; the Company are playing " Hide the Thimble" ; i.e., some-one has planted that article in a place so conspicuous that few would expect to find it there.   As each person catches sight of it, he or she sits down.   UNCLE JOSEPH is still, to the general merriment, wandering about and getting angrier every moment.*

MR. C.   That's it, Uncle, you're *warm*—you're *getting* warm!

UNCLE J. (*boiling over*).   *Warm*, Sir?   *I am* warm—and something more, I can tell you!   [*Sits down with a bump.*

MR. C.   You haven't *seen* it!   I'm sure you haven't seen it.   Come now, Uncle!

"*Warm*, SIR? I *am* WARM—AND SOMETHING MORE!"

UNCLE J. Never mind whether I have or have not. Perhaps I don't *want* to see it, Sir !

THE CHILDREN. Then do you give it up ? Do you want to be told ? Why, it's staring you in the face all the time !

UNCLE J. I don't care whether it's staring or not—I don't want to be told anything more about it.

THE CHILDREN. Then you're *cheating*, Uncle—you must go on walking till you *do* see it !

UNCLE J. Oh, that's it, eh ? Very well, then—I'll walk !

[*Walks out, leaving the company paralysed.*

MRS. C. Run after him, Tommy, and tell him—quick !

[*Exit* TOMMY.

MR. C. (*feebly*). I think when Uncle Joseph does come back, we'd better try to think of some game he *can't* lose his temper at. Ah, here's Tommy !

TOMMY. I *told* him—but he went all the same, and slammed the door. He said I was to go back and tell you that you would find he *was* cut up—and cut up rough, too !

MRS. C. But what did you tell *him* ?

TOMMY. Why, only that Parpar asked him to come to-night because he was sure to cut up well. You said I might !

[*Sensation ; Prompt departure of* TOMMY *for bed ; moralising by Aunts ; a spirit of perfect candour prevails ; names are called —also cabs ; further hostilities postponed till next Christmas.*

On the Ice.

SCENE—*The Serpentine. On the bank, several persons are having their skates put on ; practised Skaters being irritable and impatient, and others curiously the reverse, at any delay in the operation.*

CHORUS OF UNEMPLOYED SKATE-FASTENERS. 'Oo'll 'ave a pair on for an hour ? Good Sport to-day, Sir! Try a pair on, Mum! (*to any particularly stout Lady*). Will yer walk inter *my* porler, Sir ? corpet all the w'y! 'Ad the pleasure o' puttin' on your skites last year, Miss! Best skates in London, Sir! [*Exhibiting a primæval pair.*

THE USUAL COMIC COCKNEY (*to his Friend, who has undertaken to instruct him*). No '*urry*, old man—this joker ain't *arf* finished with me yet! (*To* SKATE-FASTENER.) Easy with that jimlet, Guv'nor. My 'eel ain't 'orn, like a 'orse's 'oof! If you're goin' to strap me up as toight as all that, I shell 'ave to go to *bed* in them skites! . . . Well, what is it *now* ?

SKATE-FASTENER. Reg'lar thing fur Gen'lm'n as 'ires skates ter leave somethink be'ind, jest as security like—*anythink*'ll do—a gold watch and chain, if yer got sech a thing about yer!

THE C. C. Oh, I dessay—not *me!*

SKATE-F. (*wounded*). Why, yer needn't be afroid! *I* shorn't run away—you'll find *me* 'ere when yer come back!

THE C. C. Ah, that *will* be noice! But all the sime, a watch is a thing that slips out of mind so easy, yer know. You might go and forgit all about it. 'Ere's a match-box instead ; it ain't silver!

SKATE-F. (*with respect*). Ah, you *do* know the world, *you* do!

THE C. C. Now, Alf, old man, I'm ready for yer! Give us 'old of yer 'and . . . Go slow now. What's the Vestry about not to put some gravel down 'ere? It's downright dangerous! Whoo-up! Blowed if I ain't got some other party's legs on! . . . Sloide more? Whadjer torking about! I'm sloidin' every way at once, *I* am! . . . Stroike out? I've struck sparks enough out of the back o' my 'ed, if that's all! . . . Git up? Ketch me! I'm a deal syfer settin' dayown, and I'll sty 'ere! [*He stays.*

A NERVOUS SKATER (*hobbling cautiously down the bank—to Friend*). I—I don't know how I shall *be* in these, you know—haven't had a pair on for years. (*Striking out.*) Well, come—(*relieved*)—skating's one of those things you never forget—all a question of poise and equi—confound the things! No, I'm all right, thanks—lump in the ice, that's all! As I was saying, skating soon comes back to—thought I was gone that time! Stick by me, old fellow, till I begin to feel my—Oh, hang it *all!* . . . Eh? surely we have been on more than five minutes! Worst of skating is, your feet get so cold! . . . These *are* beastly skates. Did you hear that crack? Well, *you* may stay on if you like, but I'm not going to risk *my* life for a few minutes' pleasure! [*He returns to bank.*

THE FOND MOTHER (*from bank, to* CHILDREN *on the ice*). That's right. Alma, you're doing it *beautifully*—don't *walk* so much! (*To* FRENCH GOVERNESS). Alma fay bocoo de progray, may elle ne glisse assez—nayse par, Ma'amzell?

MADEMOISELLE. C'est Ella qui est la plus habile, elle patine déjà très bien—et avec un aplomb!

THE F. M. Wee-wee; may Ella est la plus viaile, vous savvy. Look at Ella, Alma, and see how *she* does it!

MAD. Vous marchez toujours—toujours, Alma; tâchez donc de glisser un petit peu—c'est beaucoup plus facile!

ALMA. Snay pas facile quand vous avez les skates toutes sur un côté—comme *moi*, Ma'amzell!

F. M. Ne repondy à Ma'amzell, Alma, and watch Ella!

ELLA. Regardez-moi, Alma. Je puis voler vite—oh, mais vite . . . oh I *have* hurt myself so!

ALMA (*with sisterly sympathy.*) *That's* what comes of trying to show off, Ella, darling! [ELLA *is helped to the bank.*

A PATERNAL SKATE-FASTENER. 'Ere you are, Missie—set down on

"'SNAY PAS FACILE QUAND VOUS AVEZ LES SKATES TOUTES SUR UN CÔTÉ—COMME MOI!'"

this 'ere cheer—and you, too, my little dear—lor, *they* won't do them cheers no 'arm, Mum, bless their little 'arts! Lemme tyke yer little skites orf, my pooties. *I'll* be keerful, Mum—got childring o' my own at 'ome—the moral o' *your* two, Mum!

THE F. M. (*to* GOVERNESS). Sayt un homme avec un bong ker. Avez-vous—er—des cuivres, Ma'amzell?

THE P. S. (*disgustedly*). Wot?—only two bloomin' browns fur tykin' the skites orf them two kids' trotters! I want a shellin' orf o' you fur that job, *I* do . . . "Not another penny?" Well, if you do everythink as cheap as you do yer skiting, you orter be puttin' money by, *you* ought! That's right, tyke them snivellin' kids 'ome—blow me if ever I—&c. &c., &c. 　　　　　　　　　　　[*Exit party, pursued by powerful metaphors.*

THE EGOTISTIC SKATER (*in charge of a small* NIECE). Just see if you can get along by yourself a little—I'll come back presently. Practise striking out.

THE NIECE. But, Uncle, directly I strike out, I fall down!

THE E. S. (*encouragingly*). You will at first, till you get into it—gives you confidence. Keep on at it—don't stand about, or you'll catch cold. I shall be keeping my eye on you! 　　　[*Skates off to better ice.*

THE FANCY SKATER (*to less accomplished* FRIEND). This is a pretty figure—sort of variation of the "Cross Cut," ending up with "The Vine"; it's done this way (*illustrating*), quarter of circle on outside edge forwards; then sudden stop——(*He sits down with violence*). Didn't quite come off that time!

THE FRIEND. The sudden stop came off right enough, old fellow!

THE F. S. I'll show you again—it's really a neat thing when it's well done; you do it all on one leg, like this——
　　　　　　　　　　　　[*Executes an elaborate back-fall.*

HIS FRIEND. You seem to do most of it on no legs at all, old chap!

THE F. S. Haven't practised it lately, that's all. Now here's a figure I invented myself. "The Swooping Hawk" I call it.

HIS FRIEND (*unkindly—as the* F. S. *comes down in the form of a St. Andrew's Cross*). Y—yes. More like a Spread Eagle though, ain't it?

PRETTY GIRL (*to* Mr. ACKMEY, *who has been privileged to take charge*

"GO IT, OLE FRANKY, MY SON!"

of herself and her PLAIN SISTER).　Do come and tell me if I'm doing it right, Mr. Ackmey.　You *said* you'd go round with me !

THE PLAIN S.　How can you be so *selfish*, Florrie ?　You've had ever so much more practice than *I* have !　Mr. Ackmey, I wish you'd look at my left boot—it *will* go like that.　Is it my ankle—or what ?　And this strap *is* hurting me so !　Couldn't you loosen it, or take me back to the man, or something ?　Florrie can get on quite well alone, can't she ?

MR. A. (*temporising feebly*).　Er—suppose I give *each* of you a hand, eh ?

THE PLAIN S.　No ;　I can't go along fast, like you and Florrie.　You promised to look after me, and I'm perfectly helpless alone !

THE PRETTY S.　Then, am I to go by myself, Mr. Ackmey ?

MR. A.　I—I think—just for a little, if you don't mind !

THE PRETTY S.　Mind ?　Not a bit !　There's Clara Willoughby and her brother on the next ring, I'll go over to them.　Take good care of Alice, Mr. Ackmey.　Good-bye for the present.

　　　　[*She goes ;* ALICE *doesn't think* Mr. A. *is "nearly so nice as he used to be."*

THE RECKLESS ROUGH.　Now then, I'm on 'ere.　Clear the way, all of yer !　Parties must look out fur themselves when they see *me* a comin', I carn't stop fur nobody !

　　　　[*Rushes round the ring at a tremendous pace.*

AN ADMIRING SWEEPER (*following his movements with enthusiasm*).　Theer he goes—the Ornimental Skyter !　Look at 'im a buzzin' round !　Lor, it's a treat to see 'im bowlin' 'em all over like a lot er bloomin' nine-pins !　Go it, ole Franky, my son—don't you stop to apollergise ! . . . Ah, there he goes on his nut agen !　'*E* don't care, not '*e* ! . . . Orf he goes agin ! . . . That's *another* on 'em down, and ole Franky atop—'e'll 'ave the ring all to 'isself presently !　Up agin !　Oh, ain't he *lovely* !　I never see his loike afore nowheres . . . *Round* yer go—that's the stoyle !　My eyes, if he ain't upset another—a lydy this time—she's done '*er* skytin fur the d'y any 'ow !　and ole Frank knocked silly . . . Well, I ain't larfed ser much in all my life !　　　　　　　　[*He is left laughing.*

In a Fog.

(A Reminiscence of the Past Month.)

SCENE—*Main thoroughfare near Hyde Park. Time* 8 P.M. *Nothing visible anywhere, but very much audible ; horses slipping and plunging, wheels grinding, crashes, jolts, and English as she is spoke on such occasions.*

MRS. FLUSTERS (*who is seated in a brougham with her husband, on their way to dine with some friends in Cromwell Road*). We shall be dreadfully late, I know we shall ! I'm sure Peacock could go faster than this if he liked—he always loses his head when there's much traffic. Do tell him to make haste !

MR. F. Better let him alone—he knows what he's doing.

MRS. F. I don't believe he does, or he wouldn't dawdle like this. If you won't speak to him, I must. (*Lets down the glass and puts out her head.*) Peacock !

A BLURRED SHADOW ON THE BOX. Yes, M'm.

MRS. F. What are we stopping for like this ?

THE SHADOW. Fog very thick just 'ere, M'm. Can't see what's in front of us, M'm.

MRS. F. It's just as safe to keep moving as to stand still—go on at once.

THE S. Very good, M'm. (*To horse.*) Pull urp !   [*Crash !*

VOICE FROM THE UNSEEN. What the blanky blank, &c.

PEACOCK. There *is* suthin in front, M'm. A van, from 'is langwich, M'm.

MRS. F. (*sinking back*). Marmaduke, this is awful. I'd no idea the fog was like this—or I should never have —— (*With temper.*) Really, people have no *right* to ask one out on such a night.

MR. F. (*with the common sense that makes him "so aggravating at times"*). Well, Fanny, you could hardly expect 'em to foresee the weather three weeks ahead!

MRS. F. At all events, *you* might have seen what it was going to be as you came home from the Temple. Then we could have sent a telegram!

MR. F. It seemed to be lifting then, and besides, I—ah—regard a dinner-engagement as a species of kindly social contract, not to be broken except under pressing necessity.

MRS. F. You mean you heard me say there was nothing but cold meat in the house, and you know you'll get a good dinner at the Cordon-Blewitts,—not that we are likely to get there to-night. Have you any idea whereabouts we are?

MR. F. (*calmly*). None whatever.

MRS. F. Then ask Peacock.

MR. F. (*lets down his window, and leans out*). Peacock!

THE SHADOW. Sir?

MR. F. Where have we got to now?

PEACOCK. I ain't rightly sure, Sir.

MRS. F. Tell him to turn round, and go home.

MR. F. It's no use going on like this. Turn back.

PEACOCK. I dursn't leave the kerb—all I got to go by, Sir.

MR. F. Then take one of the lamps, and lead the horse.

PEACOCK. It's the *young* 'orse, Sir.

MR. F. (*sinking back*). We must put up with it, I suppose.

[*A smart crack is heard at the back of the carriage.*

MORE VOICES. Now, then, why the blanky dash, &c., &c.

MRS. F. Marmaduke, I can't sit here, and know that a bus-pole may come between us at any moment. Let us get out, and take a cab home at once.

MR. F. There's only one objection to that suggestion—viz., that it's perfectly impossible to tell a cab from a piano-organ. We must find out where we are first, and then turn. Peacock, drive on as well as you can, and stop when you come to a shop.

MRS. F. What do you want to stop at a shop for?

MR. F. Why, then I can go in, and ask where we *are.*

MRS. F. And how do you expect *them* to know where we are! (*She sees a smear of light in the distance.*) Marmaduke, there's a linkman. Get out quick, and hire him to lead the way.

MR. F. (*who gets out, and follows in the direction of the light, grumbling to himself*). Hallo!—not past the park yet—here's the railings! Well, if I keep close to them, I shall—(*He suddenly collides with a bench*). Phew! Oh, confound it! (*He rubs his shins.*) Now, if it hadn't been for Fanny, I — Where's that linkman? Hi!—you there!—stop! (*The light stops.*) Look here—I want you to come to my carriage, and show my man the way out of this!

VOICE FROM BEHIND THE RAILINGS. We got to find our *own* way out fust, Guv'nor. We're *inside!*

A BELATED REVELLER (*lurching up to* MR. F.) Beg your pardon, bur cou' you dreck me nearesht way—er—Dawshon Plashe?

MR. F. (*savagely*). First turning to the right, third to the left, and then straight on till you come to it!

THE B. R. I'm exsheedingly 'blished; (*confidentially*) fact ish, I'm shuffrin' shli' 'fection eyeshi', an' I 'shure you, can't shee anyshing dishtingly to-ni'. (*He cannons against a lamp-post, to which he clings affectionately, as a Policeman emerges from the gloom.*)

POLICEMAN. Now then, what are you doing 'ere, eh?

THE B. R. Itsh all ri', P'lishman, thish gerrilman—(*patting lamp-post affectionately*)—has kindly promished shee me home.

MR. F. Hang it! Where's Peacock and the brougham? (*He discovers a phantom vehicle by the kerb, and gets in angrily.*) Now, look here, my dear, it's no earthly good—!

OCCUPANT OF THE BROUGHAM (*who is not* FANNY). Coward, touch a defenceless woman if you dare! I have nothing on me of any value. Help! Police!

[MR. F., *seeing that explanation is useless, lets himself out again, precipitately, dodges the* POLICEMAN, *and bolts, favoured by the fog, until all danger of pursuit is passed, at the end of which time he suddenly realizes that it is perfectly hopeless to attempt to find his own carriage again. He gropes his way home, and some hours later, after an extemporised cold supper, is rejoined by his Wife.*

MRS. F. (*cheerfully*). So *there* you are, Marmaduke! I wasn't anxious —I felt sure you'd find your way back somehow!

MR. F. (*not in the best of tempers*). Find my way back! It was the only thing I could do. But where have *you* been all this time, Fanny?

MRS. F. Where? Why, at the Blewitts, to be sure. You see, after you got out, we had to keep moving on, and by and by the fog got better, and we could see where we were going to,—and the Blewitts had put off dinner half an hour, so I was not so *very* late. Such a *nice* dinner! Everybody turned up except *you*, Marmaduke—but I *told* them how it was. Oh, and old Lady Horehound was there, and said a man had actually got into her brougham, and tried to wrench off one of her most valuable bracelets!—only she spoke to him so severely that he was struck with remorse, or something, and got out again! And it was by the Park, *close* to where you left me. Just fancy, Marmaduke, he might have got into the carriage with *me*, instead!

MR. F. (*gloomily*). Yes, he *might*—only, he—er—*didn't*, you know!

Bricks without Straw.

SCENE—*A Village School-room. A Juvenile Treat is in progress, and a Magic Lantern, hired for the occasion, " with set of slides complete—to last one hour," is about to be exhibited.*

THE VICAR'S DAUGHTER (*suddenly recognizing the New Curate, who is blinking unsuspectingly in the lantern rays*). Oh, Mr. Tootler, you've just come in time to help us! The man with the lantern says he only manages the slides, and can't do the talking part. And I've asked lots of people, and no one will volunteer. *Would* you mind just explaining the pictures to the children? It's only a little Nursery tale —*Valentine and Orson*—I chose that, because it's less hackneyed, and has such an excellent *moral*, you know. I'm sure you'll do it so *beautifully !*

MR. TOOTLER (*a shy man*). I—I'd do it with pleasure, I'm sure— only I really don't know anything about *Valentine and Orson !*

THE V.'s D. Oh, what *does* that matter? I can tell you the outline in two minutes. (*She tells him.*) But it's got to last an hour, so you must spin it out as much as ever you can.

MR. TOOTLER (*to himself*). Ought I to neglect such a golden opportunity of winning these young hearts? No. (*Aloud.*) I will—er—do my best, and perhaps I had better begin at once, as they seem to be getting— er—rather unruly at the further end of the room. (*He clears his throat.*) Children, you must be very quiet and attentive, and then we shall be able, as we purpose this evening, to show you some scenes illustrative of the—

er—beautiful old story of *Valentine and Orson*, which I doubt not is familiar to you all. (*Rustic applause, conveyed by stamping and shrill cheers, after which a picture is thrown on the screen representing a Village Festival.*) Here, children, we have a view of—er—(*with sudden inspiration*)— Valentine's Native Village. It is—er—his birthday, and Valentine, being a young man who is universally beloved on account of his amiability and good conduct—(*To the* VICAR'S D. " Is that correct ?" THE V.'s D. " Quite, *quite* correct ! ")—good conduct, the villagers are celebrating the —er—auspicious event by general rejoicings. How true it is that if we are only *good*, we may, young as we are, count upon gaining the affection and esteem of all around us! (*A Youthful Rustic, with a tendency to heckle.* " Ef 'ee plaze, Zur, which on 'em be Valentoine ?") Valentine, we may be very sure, would not be absent on such an occasion, although, owing to the crowd, we cannot distinguish him. But, wherever he is, how- ever he may be occupied, he little thinks that, before long, he will have to encounter the terrible Orson, the Wild Man of the Woods! Ah, dear children, we all have our Wild Man of the Woods to fight. With *some of us* it is—(*He improves the occasion*). Our next picture represents—(*To* ASSISTANT). Sure this comes next ? Oh, they're all numbered, are they ? Very well—represents a forest—er—the home of Orson. If we were permitted to peep behind one of those trunks, we should doubtless see Orson himself, crouching in readiness to spring upon the unsuspecting Valentine. So, often when we—&c., &c. The next scene we shall show you represents the—er—burning of Valentine's ship. Valentine has gone on a voyage, with the object of—er—finding Orson. If the boat in the picture was only larger, we could no doubt identify Valentine, sitting there undismayed, calmly confident that, notwithstanding this—er— unfortunate interruption, he will be guided, sooner or later, to his—er— goal. Yes, dear children, if we only have patience, if we only have faith, &c., &c. Here we see—(*an enormous Bison is suddenly depicted on the screen*) eh ? oh, yes—here we have a specimen of—er—Orson's *pursuits*. He chases the bison. Some of you may not know what a bison is. It is a kind of hairy cow, and—(*He describes the habits of these creatures as fully as he is able.* (THE YOUTHFUL RUSTIC. "Theer baint nawone a-erntin' of 'un, Zur.") What? Oh, but there *is*, you know. Orson is pursuing him, only—er—the bison, being a very fleet animal, has outrun his pursuer for the moment. Sometimes we flatter ourselves that we have outrun *our* pursuer—but, depend upon it, &c., &c. But now let us see what Valentine is about—(*Discovering, not without surprise, that the next picture is a Scene in the Arctic Regions*). Well, you see, he has succeeded in reaching the coast, and here he is—in a sledge drawn by a reindeer, with nothing to guide him but the Aurora Borealis, hastening towards the spot where he has been told he will find Orson. He doesn't despair, doesn't lose heart—he is sure that, if he only keeps on, if he—er—only continues, only perseveres —(*Aside.* What drivel I *am* talking! *To* ASSISTANT. I say, are there many *more* of this sort? because we *don't* seem to be getting on!)—Well, now we come to—(*a Moonlight Scene, with a Cottage in Winter, appears*) —to the—ah—home of Valentine's *mother.* You will observe a light in the casement. By that light the good old woman is sitting, longing and praying for the return of her gallant boy. Ah, dear children, what a thing a good old mother is! (*To the* VICAR'S DAUGHTER.) " I really can *not* keep on like this much longer. I'm positively certain these slides are out of order!" THE V.'S D. " Oh, no; I'm sure it's *all* right. Do *please* go on. They're *so* interested!" THE YOUNG HECKLER. "'Ow 'bout Valentoine, Zur?—wheer be 'ee?" Ah, where is Valentine, indeed? (*To* ASS.) Next slide—quick! (*Recognises with dismay a View of the Grand Canal.*) No— but, I say—*really, I can't*— Here we have Valentine at Venice. He has reached that beautiful city,—well called the Queen of the Adriatic,—at last! He contemplates it from his gondola, and yet he has no heart just now to take in all the beauty of the scene. He feels that he is still no nearer to finding Orson than before. (THE YOUNG HECKLER. " Naw moor be we, Zur. We ain't zeed *nayther* on 'em zo fur!" *Tumult, and a general demand for the instant production of Orson or Valentine.*) Now, children, children! this is very irregular. You must allow me to tell this story my own way. I assure you that you will see them both in good time, if you only keep still! (*To* ASS.) I can't stand this any more

RECOGNISES WITH DISMAY A VIEW OF THE GRAND CANAL.

Valentine and Orson must be underneath the rest. Find them, and shove them in quick. Never mind the numbering! (*The screen remains blank while the* ASSISTANT *fumbles.*) Well, have you *got* them?

THE ASSISTANT. No, Sir; I'm rather afraid they ain't *here*. Fact is, they've sent me out with the wrong set o' slides. This ain't *Valentine and Orson—it's a miscellaneous lot, Sir!*

[*Collapse of Curate as Scene closes in.*

At a Music Hall.

SCENE.—*The auditorium of a Music Hall, the patrons of which are respectable, but in no sense " smart."   The occupants of the higher-priced seats appear to have dropped in less for the purpose of enjoying the entertainment than of discussing their private affairs—though this does not prevent them from applauding everything with generous impartiality.*

THE CHAIRMAN.   Ladies and Gentlemen, the Celebrated Character-Duettists and Variety Artistes, the Sisters Silvertwang, will appear next !
> [*They do ; they have just sung a duet in praise of Nature with an interspersed step-dance. " Oh, I love to 'ear the echo on the Moun-ting !" (Tiddity-iddity-iddity-iddity-um !) " And to listen to the tinkle of the Foun-ting !" (Tiddity, &c.)*

A WHITE-CAPPED ATTENDANT (*taking advantage of a pause, plaintively*).   Sengwidges, too-pence !

VOLUBLE LADY *in the Shilling Stalls* (*telling her Male Companion an interminable story with an evasive point*).   No, but you 'ear what I'm going to *tell* you, because I'm coming to it presently.   I can't remember his name at this moment—something like Budkin, but it wasn't that, somewhere near Bond Street, he is, or a street off there ; a Scotchman, but *that* doesn't matter ! (*Here she breaks off to hum the Chorus of " Good Ole Mother-in-Law !" which is being sung on the stage.*)   Well, let me see —what was I telling you ?   Wait a minute, excuse *me*, oh, yes,—*well*, there was this picture,—mind you, it's a lovely *painting*, but the frame simply nothing,—not that I go by frames, myself, o' course not, but I fetched it down to show him—oh, I know what you'll say, but he must know *something* about such things ; he knew my uncle, and I can tell you what he *is*—he's a florist, and married nineteen years, and his wife's forty—years older than me, but I've scarcely spoke to *her*, and no children, so I fetched it to show him, and as soon as he sets eyes on it, he says——(FEMALE

THE SISTERS SILVERTWANG.

"CHARACTER-COMIC" *on Stage, lugubriously.* "Ritoldcriddle, ol de*ray* ritoldcriddle, olde-*ri-ido !*") I can't tell you *how* old it is, but 'undreds of years, and Chinese, I shouldn't wonder, but we can't trace its 'istry—that's what *he* said, and if *he* don't know, *nobody* does, for it stands to reason he must be a judge, though nothing to me,—when I say nothing, I mean all I know of him is that he used to be—— (TENOR VOCALIST ON STAGE. " My Sweetheart when a Bo-oy!") I always like that song, don't you ? Well, and this is what I was *wanting* to tell you, *she* got to know what I'd done —how is more'n *I* can tell you, but she did, and she come straight in to where I was, and I see in a minute she'd been drinking, for drink she does, from morning to night, but I don't mind *that*, and her bonnet all on the back of her head, and her voice that 'usky, she—— (TENOR. " She sang a Song of Home Sweet Home—a song that reached my heart !") And I couldn't be expected to put up with *that*, you know, but I haven't 'alf told you yet—*well*, &c., &c.

IN THE RESERVED STALLS.

FIRST PROFESSIONAL LADY, "*resting*," to SECOND DITTO (*as* MISS FLORRIE FOLJAMBE *appears on Stage*). New dresses to-night.

SECOND DITTO. Yes. (*Inspects* MISS F.'s *costume.*) Something wrong with that boy's dress in front, though, cut too low. Is that silver bullion it's trimmed with ? That silver stuff they put on my pantomime-dress has turned quite yellow !

FIRST DITTO. It will sometimes. Did you know any of the critics when you were down at Slagtown for the Panto ?

SECOND DITTO. I knew the *Grimeshire Mercury*, and he said most awfully rude things about me in his paper. I was rather rude to him at rehearsal, but we made it up afterwards. You know Lily's married, dear ?

FIRST DITTO. What—Lily ? You don't mean it !

SECOND DITTO. Oh, yes, she *is*, though. She went out to Buenos Ayres, and the other day she was taken in to dinner by the Bishop of the Friendly Islands.

FIRST DITTO. A Bishop ? *Fancy !* That *is* getting on, isn't it ?

MISS FOLJAMBE (*on Stage, acknowledging an encore*). Ladies and Gentlemen, I am very much obliged for your kind reception this evening, but having been lately laid up with a bad cold, and almost entirely lost my voice, and being still a little 'orse, I feel compelled to ask your kind acceptance of a few 'ornpipe steps, after which I 'ope to remain, Ladies and Gentlemen, always your obedient 'umble servant to command—Florrie Foljambe!

> [*Tumultuous applause, and hornpipe.*

CHAIRMAN. Professor Boodler, the renowned Imitator of Birds, will appear next!

THE PROFESSOR (*on Stage*). Ladies and Gentlemen, I shall commence by an attempt to give you an imitation of that popular and favourite songster the Thrush—better known to some of you, I dare say, as the Throstle, or Mavis! (*He gives the Thrush—which somehow doesn't "go."*) I shall next endeavour to represent that celebrated and tuneful singing-bird—the Sky-lark. (*He does it, but the Lark doesn't quite come off.*) I shall next try to give you those two sweet singers, the Male and Female Canary—the gentleman in the stalls with the yellow 'air will represent the female bird on this occasion, he must not be offended, for it is a 'igh compliment I am paying him, a harmless professional joke. (*The Canaries obtain but tepid acknowledgments.*) I shall now conclude my illustrations of bird-life with my celebrated imitation of a waiter drawing the cork from a bottle of gingerbeer, and drinking it afterwards.

> [*Does so; rouses the audience to frantic enthusiasm, and retires after triple recall.*

THE VOLUBLE LADY *in the Shilling Stalls* (*during the performance of a Thrilling Melodramatic Sketch*). I've nothing to say against her 'usban', a quiet, respectable man, and always treated *me* as a lady, with grey whiskers—but that's neither here nor there—and I speak of parties as I find them—*well. That* was a Thursday. On the *Saturday* there came a knock at my door, and I answered it, and there was she saying, as cool as you please—— (HEROINE ON STAGE. "Ah, no, no—you would not ruin me? You will not tell my husband?") So I told her. "I'm very sorry," I says, "but I can't lend that frying-pan to nobody." So I got up. Two hours *after*, as I was going down stairs, she come out of her room, and says,—"'Allo, Rose, 'ow *are* yer?" as if nothing had 'appened. "Oh, jolly," I says, or somethink o' that sort—*I* wasn't going to take no notice of *her*—and she says, "Going out?"—like that. I says, "Oh, yes; nothing to stay in for," I says, careless-like; so Mrs. Piper, *she* never said nothing, and *I* didn't say nothing ; and so it went on till Monday—*well!* Her 'usban' met me in the passage ; and he said to me—good-tempered and civil enough, I *must* say—he said—— (VILLAIN ON STAGE. "Curse you! I've had enough of this fooling! Give me money, or I'll twist your neck, and fling you into yonder mill-dam, to drown !") So o' course I'd no objection to that ; and all she wanted, in the way of eatables and drink, she '*ad*—no, let me finish *my* story first. Well, just fancy '*er* now! She asked me to step in ; and she says, " Ow are you ?" and was very nice, and I never said a word—not wishing to bring up the past, and—I didn't tell you *this*—they'd a kind of old easy chair in the room—and the only remark *I* made, not meaning anythink, was—— (HERO ON STAGE. "You infernal, black-hearted scoundrel! this is *your* work, is it ?") Well, I couldn't ha' put it more pleasant than that, *could* I ? and old Mr. Fitkin, as was settin' on it, he says to me, he says—— (HERO. "Courage, my darling! You shall not perish if my strong arms can save you. Heaven help me to rescue the woman I love better than my life !") but he's 'alf silly, so I took no partickler notice of '*im*, when, what did that woman do, after stoopin' to me, as she 'as, times without number—but— Oh, is the play over ? Well, as I was saying—oh, *I'm* ready to go if you are, and I can tell you the rest walking home.   [*Exit, having thoroughly enjoyed her evening.*

A Recitation under Difficulties.

SCENE.—*An Evening Party;* MISS FRESIA BLUDKINSON, *a talented young Professional Reciter, has been engaged to entertain the company, and is about to deliver the favourite piece entitled, "The Lover of Lobelia Bangs, a Cowboy Idyl." There is the usual crush, and the guests outside the drawing-room, who can neither hear nor see what is going on, console themselves by conversing in distinctly audible tones. Jammed in a doorway, between the persons who are trying to get in, and the people who would be only too glad to get out, is an* UNSOPHISTICATED GUEST *who doesn't know a soul, and is consequently reduced to listening to the Recitation. This is what he hears:—*

MISS FRESIA BLUD. (*in a tone of lady-like apology*).

I am only a Cowboy——

> [*Several Ladies put up their glasses, and examine her critically, as if they had rather expected this confession. Sudden burst of Society Chatter from without.*

SOCIETY CHATTER. How d'ye do? . . . Oh, but her parties never *are !* . . . How are you? . . . No, I left her at . . . Yes, he's somewhere about . . . Saw you in the Row this mornin' . . . Are you doing anything on——? . . . Oh, *what* a shame! . . . No, but *doesn't* she now? . . . No earthly use trying to get in at present . . . &c., &c.

MISS FRESIA B. (*beginning again, with meek despair, a little louder*).

I am only a Cowboy; reckless, rough, in an unconventional suit of clothes ;
I hain't, as a rule, got much to say, and my conversation is mostly oaths.

[Cries of " Ssh !" intended, however, for the people outside, who are chattering harder than ever.

When the cackle of females strikes my ear——

SOCIETY CHATTER (*as before*). Oh, *much* cooler here . . . Yes, delightful, wasn't it ? Everybody one knows . . . No, you don't *really ?* . . . Oh, Popsy's flourishing, thanks . . . The new Butler turned out a perfect demon. . . . but I said I wouldn't have his tail docked for anything . . . so they've painted it *eau de Nil*, and it looks *so* nice !

MISS F. B. (*pointedly*).

When the cackle of females strikes my ear, I jest vamose, for they make me skeered, And I sorter suspicion I skeer them too, with my hulking form, and my bushy beard !

[Here, of course, she strokes a very round chin.

SOCIETY CHATTER. Seems to be somethin' goin' on in there—singin', actin', dancin', or somethin' . . . Well, of course, only heard *her* version of it as yet, y' know . . . Have you seen him in . . . white bengaline with a Medici collar, and one of those . . . nasty gouty attacks he *will* have are only rheumatism, &c., &c.

MISS F. B. (*when next heard*).

I cleared my throat and I tried to speak—but the words died strangled—

A FEMININE VOICE OUTSIDE. So *long* since we had a quiet talk together ! Do tell me all about, &c., &c.

MISS F. B.   ——strangled by sheer alarm.

For there in front——

[Here she points dramatically at a stout matron, who fans herself consciously.

——was the slender form, and the sweet girl-face of our new " School Marm " !

Say, boys ! hev' ye heard an Æolian harp which a Zephyr's tremulous finger twangs ? Wa'al, it kinder thrills ye the way I felt when I first beheld Lobelia Bangs !

SOC. CHAT. Oh, you really *ought* to go—so touching ! Dick and I both regularly howled all through the last act . . . Not in the *least*, thanks. Well, if there *is* a seat . . . You're sure there *are* any ices ? Then, strawberry, please—no, *nothing* to drink ! . . . *Will* you allow me ?

"I AM ONLY A COWBOY."

. . . Told she could dress hair perfectly, but I soon found she was . . . a Swedenborgian, my dear, or something horrid . . . Haven't you? *I've* had it three times, and . . . so many people have asked me for cards that really I . . . had the drains thoroughly looked to, and now they're . . . delicious, but rather overpowering in a *room*, I think! &c., &c.

MISS F. B. (*with genuine feeling*).

Who would imagine one meek-voiced girl could have held her own in a deafening din!
But Lobelia's scholars discovered soon she'd a dead-sure notion of discipline;
For her satin palm had a sting like steel, and the rowdiest rebel respected her,
When she'd stretched out six of the hardest lots in the Bible-Class with a Derringer!

SOC. CHAT. No, a very dull party, you could move about quite easily in all the rooms, so we . . . kicked the whole concern to shivers and . . . came on here as soon as we could . . . Capital dinner they *gave* us too . . . &c., &c.

MISS F. B. (*with as much conviction as possible under the circumstances*).

And the silence deepened; no creature stirred in the stagnant hush, and the only sound
Was the far-off lumbering jolt, produced by the prairie rolling for leagues around!

SOC. CHAT. (*crescendo*). Oh, an old aunt of mine has gone in for step-dancing—she's had several lessons . . . and cut her knees rather badly, y' know, so I put her out to grass . . . and now she can sit up and hold a biscuit on her nose . . . but she really ought to mix a little grey in her wig!

[*&c., &c., to the distraction of the* UNSOPHISTICATED GUEST, *who is getting quite interested in Lobelia Bangs, whom he suddenly discovers, much to his surprise, on horseback.*

MISS F. B.

And on we cantered, without a word, in the mid-day heat, on our swift mustangs.
I was only ignorant Cowboy Clem—but I worshipped bright Lobelia Bangs!

SOC. CHAT. (*fortissimo*). Not for ages; but last time I met him he was . . . in a dreadful state, with the cook down with influenza . . . and so I suppose he's *married* her by this time!

MISS F. B. (*excitedly*).

But hark! in the distance a weird shrill cry, a kinder mournful, monotonous yelp—
(*Further irruption of* SOCIETY CHATTER) . . . is it jackal?—bison?—a cry for help.)

Soc. Chat. Such a complete *rest*, you know—so perfectly peaceful! Not a soul to talk to. I *love* it . . . but, to really enjoy a tomato, you must see it dressed . . . in the *sweetest* little sailor suit!

Miss F. B.

My horse was a speck on the pampas' verge, for I dropped the rein in my haste to stoop;
Then I pressed my ear to the baking soil—and caught—ah, horror—the Indian whoop!

Soc. Chat. Some say it *isn't* infectious, but one can't be too careful, and, with children in the house, &c., &c.

Miss F. B.

I rose to my feet with quivering knees, and my face went white as a fresh-washed towel;
I had heard a war-cry I knew too well—'twas the murderous bellow of Blue-nosed Owl!

Soc. Chat. Nice fellow—I'm very fond of him—so fresh—capital company—met him when I was over there, &c.

Miss F. B.

"What! leave you to face those fiends alone!" she cried, and slid from her horse's back;
"Let me die with you—for I love you, Clem!" Then she gave her steed a resounding smack,
And he bounded off; "Now Heaven be praised that my school six-shooter I brought!" said she.
"Four barrels I'll keep for the front-rank foes—and the next for you—and the last for me!"

Soc. Chat. Is it a *comic* piece she's doing, do you know? Don't think so, I can see somebody smiling. Sounds rather like Shakespeare, or Dickens, or one of those fellahs . . . Didn't catch what you said. No. Quite impossible to hear one's self speak, *isn't* it?

Miss F. B.

And ever louder the demons yelled for their pale-faced prey—but I scorned death's pangs,
For I deemed it a doom that was half delight to die by the hand of Lobelia Bangs!
Then she whispered low in her dulcet tones, like the crooning coo of a cushat dove!
(*At the top of her voice.*) "Forgive me, Clem, but I could not bear any squaw to torture my own true love!"
And she raised the revolver—"crack-crack-crack!"

[*To the infinite chagrin of the* UNSOPHISTICATED GUEST, *who is intensely anxious to hear how Miss Bangs and her lover escaped from so unpleasant a dilemma—the remaining cracks of her revolver, together with the two next stanzas, are drowned in a fresh torrent of small-talk—after which he hears* MISS F. B. *conclude with repressed emotion :*

But the ochre on Blue-nosed Owl was blurred, as his braves concluded their brief harangues ;
And he dropped a tear on the early bier of our Prairie Belle, Lobelia Bangs !

[*Which of course leaves him in a state of hopeless mystification.*
SOC. CHAT.   Is that the *end?*   Charming!   Now we shall be able to *talk* again! &c., &c.

Bank Holiday.

SCENE—*The Crystal Palace. The Nave is filled with a dense throng of Pleasure-seekers. Every free seat commanding the most distant view of a Variety Performance on the Great Stage has been occupied an hour in advance. The less punctual stand and enjoy the spectacle of other persons' hats or bonnets. Gangs of Male and Female Promenaders jostle and hustle to their hearts' content, or perform the war-song and dance of the Lower-class 'Arry, which consists in chanting "Oi tiddly-oi-toi; hoi-toi-oi!" to a double shuffle. Tired women sit on chairs and look at nothing. In the Grounds, the fancy of young men and maidens is lightly turning to thoughts of love; the first dawn of the tender passion being intimated, on the part of the youth, by chasing his charmer into a corner and partially throttling her, whereupon the maiden coyly conveys that his sentiments are not unreciprocated by thumping him between the shoulders. From time to time, two champions contend with fists for the smiles of beauty, who may usually be heard bellowing with perfect impartiality in the background. A small but increasing percentage have already had as much liquid refreshment as is good for them, and intend to have more. Altogether, the scene, if festive, might puzzle an Intelligent Foreigner who is more familar with Continental ideas of enjoyment.*

A DAMSEL (*in a ruby plush hat with a mauve feather*). Why, if they yn't got that bloomin' ole statute down from Charin' Cross! What's 'e doin' of down 'ere, I wonder?

HER SWAIN (*whose feather is only pink and white paper*). Doin' of? Tykin' 'is d'y orf—like the rest of us are tykin' it.

THE DAMSEL (*giggling*). You go on—you don't green *me* that w'y—a statute!

SWAIN. Well, 'yn't this what they call a "Statutory" 'Oliday, eh?

DAMSEL (*in high appreciation of his humour*). I'll fetch you *sech* a slap in a minnit! 'Ere, let's gow on the Swissback.

ANOTHER DAMSEL (*in a peacock-blue hat with orange pompons*). See that nekked young man on the big 'orse, ALF? It says "Castor" on the stand. 'Oo was *'e?*

ALF. Oh, *I* d'know. I dessay it 'll be 'im as invented the Castor Ile.

THE DAMSEL (*disgusted*). Fancy their puttin' up a monument to *'im!*

SUPERIOR 'ARRY (*talking Musichalls to his Adored One*). 'Ave you 'eard her sing "Come where the Booze is Cheapest?"

THE ADORED. Lots o' toimes. I *do* like *'er* singing. She mykes sech comical soigns—and then the *things* she sez! But I've 'eard she's very common in her tork, and that—*orf* the styge.

THE S. A. I shouldn't wónder. Some on 'em *are* that way. You can't 'ave *everythink!*

HIS ADORED. No, it *is* a pity, though. 'Spose we go out, and pl'y Kiss in the Ring? [*They do.*

AMONG THE ETHNOLOGICAL MODELS.

WIFE OF BRITISH WORKMAN (*spelling out placard under Hottentot Group*). "It is extremely probable that this interesting race will be completely exterminated at no very distant period." Pore things!

BRITISH WORKMAN (*with philosophy*). Well, *I* sha'n't go inter mournin' for 'em, Sairer!

LAMBETH LARRIKIN (*in a pasteboard "pickelhaube," and a false nose, thoughtfully, to* BATTERSEA BILL, *who is wearing an old grey chimney-pot hat, with the brim uppermost, and a tow wig, as they contemplate a party of Botocudo natives*). Rum the sights these 'ere savidges make o' theirselves, ain't it, Bill?

BATT. BILL (*more thoughtfully*). Yer right—but I dessay if you and me 'ad been born among that lot, *we* shouldn't care 'ow we looked!

VAUXHALL VOILET (*who has exchanged headgear with* CHELSEA CHORLEY—*with dismal results*). They *are* cures, those b!ackies! Why,

yer carn't 'ardly tell the men from the wimmin! I expect this lot 'll be
'aving a beanfeast. See, they're plyin' their myusic.

CHELSEA CHORLEY. Good job we can't *ear* 'em. They say as

"RUM THE SIGHTS THESE 'ERE SAVIDGES MAKE O' THEIRSELVES."

niggers' music is somethink downright horful. Give us "Hi-tiddly-hi" on
that mouth-orgin o' yours, will yer?

    [VAUXHALL VOILET *obliges on that instrument ; every one in the*
        neighbourhood begins to jig mechanically ; exeunt party,
        dancing.

A PIMPLY YOUTH. "Hopium-eater from Java." That's the stuff they gits as stoopid as biled howls on—it's about time we went and did another beer. [*They retire for that purpose.*

DURING THE FIREWORKS.

CHORUS OF SPECTATORS. There's another lot o' bloomin' rockets gowin orf! Oo-oo, 'ynt that lur-uvly? What a lark if the sticks come down on somebody's 'ed! There, didyer see 'em bust? Puts me in mind of a shower o' foiry smuts. Lor, so they do—what a fancy you *do* 'ave. &c., &c.

COMING HOME.

AN OLD GENTLEMAN (*who has come out with the object of observing Bank Holiday manners—which he has done from a respectful distance—to his friend, as they settle down in an empty first-class compartment*). There, now we shall just get comfortably off before the crush begins. Now, to *me*, y' know, this has been a most interesting and gratifying experience—wonderful spectacle, all that immense crowd, enjoying itself in its own way—boisterously, perhaps, but, on the whole, with marvellous decorum! Really, very exhilarating to see—but you don't agree with me?

HIS FRIEND (*reluctantly*). Well, I must say it struck me as rather pathetic than——

THE O. G. (*testily*). Pathetic, Sir—nonsense! I like to see people putting their *heart* into it, whether it's play or work. Give me a crowd——

[*As if in answer to this prayer, there is a sudden irruption of typical Bank Holiday-makers into the compartment.*

MAN BY THE WINDOW. Third-class as good as fust, these days! Why, if there ain't ole Fred! Wayo, Fred, tumble in, ole son—room for one more standin'!

["OLE FRED" *plays himself in with a triumphal blast on a tin trumpet, after which he playfully hammers the roof with his stick, as he leans against the door.*

OLE FRED. Where's my blanky friend? I 'it 'im one on the jaw, and I ain't seen 'im since! (*Sings, sentimentally, at the top of a naturally powerful voice.*) "Comrides, Com-rides! Hever since we was boys! Sharin' each other's sorrers. Sharin' each hother's—beer!"

> [*A "paraprosdokian," which delights him to the point of repetition.*]

THE O. G. Might I ask you to make a little less disturbance there, Sir? [*Whimpers from over-tired children.*]

OLE FRED (*roaring*). "I'm jolly as a Sandboy, I'm 'appy as a king! No matter what I see or 'ear, I larf at heverything! I'm the morril of my moth-ar, (*to* O. G.) the himage of *your* Par! And heverythink I see or 'ear, it makes me larf 'Ar-har!'"

> [*He laughs "Ar-har," after which he gives a piercing blast upon the trumpet, with stick obbligato on the roof.*]

THE O. G. (*roused*). I really *must* beg you not to be such an infernal nuisance! There are women and children here who——

OLE FRED. Shet up, old umbereller whiskers! (*Screams of laughter from women and children, which encourage him to sing again.*) "An' the roof is copper-bottomed, but the chimlies are of gold. In my double-breasted mansion in the Strand!" (*To people on platform, as train stops.*) *Come* in, oh, lor, *do!* "Oi-tiddly-oi-toi! hoi-toi-oy!"

> [*The rest take up the refrain—"'Ave a drink an' wet your eye," &c. and beat time with their boots.*]

THE O. G. If this abominable noise goes on, I shall call the guard—disgraceful, coming in drunk like this!

THE MAN BY THE WINDOW. 'Ere, dry up, Guv'nor—'e ain't 'ad enough to urt 'im, 'e ain't!

CHORUS OF FEMALES (*to* O. G.). An' Bank 'Oliday, too—you orter to be *ashimed* o' yerself, you ought! 'E's as right as right, if you on'y let him alone!

OLE FRED (*to* O. G.). Ga-arn, yer pore-'arted ole choiner boy! (*sings dismally*), "Ow! for the vanished Spring-toime! Ow! for the dyes gorn boy! Ow! for the"—(*changing the melody*)—"'omeless, I wander in lonely distress. No one ter pity me—none ter caress!" (*Here he sheds tears,*

overcome by his own pathos, but presently cheers up.)   " I dornce all noight!
An' I rowl 'ome toight!   I'm a rare-un at a rollick, or I'm ready fur a
foight."   Any man 'ere wanter foight me ?   Don't say no, ole Frecklefoot!
(*To the* O. G., *who perspires freely.*)   " Oh, I *am* enj'yin' myself!"

> [*He keeps up this agreeable rattle, without intermission, for the
> remainder of the journey, which—as the train stops everywhere,
> and takes quite three-quarters of an hour in getting from
> Queen's Road, Battersea, to Victoria—affords a signal proof
> of his social resources, if it somewhat modifies the* O. G.'s
> *enthusiasm for the artless gaiety of a Bank Holiday.*

A Row in the Pit; or, The Obstructive Hat.

SCENE—*The Pit during Pantomime Time. The Overture is beginning.*

AN OVER-HEATED MATRON (*to her Husband*). Well, they don't give you much *room* in 'ere, I *must* say. Still, we done better than I expected, after all that crushing. I thought my ribs was gone once—but it was on'y the umberella's. You pretty comfortable where *you* are, eh, Father?

FATHER. Oh, I'm right enough, I am.

JIMMY (*their Son; a small, bullet-headed boy, with a piping voice*). If *Father* is, it's more nor what *I* am. I can't see nothen, I can't!

HIS MOTHER. Lor' bless the boy! there ain't nothen to *see* yet; you'll see well enough when the Curting goes up. (*Curtain rises on opening scene.*) Look, Jimmy, ain't *that* nice, now? All them himps dancin' round, and real fire comin' out of the pot—which I 'ope it's quite safe—and there's a beautiful fairy just come on, dressed so grand, too!

JIMMY. I can't see no fairy—nor yet no himps—nor nothen!

[*He whimpers.*

HIS MOTHER (*annoyed*). Was there ever such a aggravating boy to take anywheres! Set quiet, do, and don't fidget, and look at the hactin'!

JIMMY. I tell yer I can't *see* no hactin', Mother. It ain't my fault—it's this lady in front o' me, with the 'at.

MOTHER (*perceiving the justice of his complaints*). Father, the pore boy says he can't see where he is, 'cause of a lady's 'at in front.

FATHER (*philosophically*). Well, *I* can't 'elp the 'at, can I? He must put up with it, that's all!

MOTHER. No—but I thought, if you wouldn't mind changing places with him—you're taller than him, and it wouldn't be in your way 'arf so much.

FATHER. It's always the way with you—never satisfied, *you* ain't!
Well, pass the boy across—I'm for a quiet life, I am. (*Changing seats.*)
Will *this* do for you?

> [*He settles down immediately behind a very large, furry, and
> feathery hat, which he dodges for some time, with the result of
> obtaining an occasional glimpse of a pair of legs on the stage.*

FATHER (*suddenly*).   D——the 'at!

"THE OWNER OF THE HAT DEIGNS NO REPLY."

MOTHER.   You can't wonder at the *boy* not seeing! P'raps the lady
wouldn't mind taking it off, if you asked her?

FATHER. Ah! (*He touches* THE OWNER OF THE HAT *on the shoulder.*)
Excuse me, Mum, but might I take the liberty of asking you to kindly
remove your 'at?   [THE OWNER OF THE HAT *deigns no reply.*

FATHER (*more insistently*).   *Would* you 'ave any objection to oblige me
by taking off your 'at, Mum? (*Same result.*) I don't know if you 'eard me,

Mum, but I've asked you twice, civil enough, to take that 'at of yours off (*pathetically*). I'm a playin' 'Ide and Seek be'ind it 'ere! [*No answer.*

THE MOTHER. People didn't ought to be allowed in the Pit with sech 'ats! Callin' 'erself a lady—and settin' there in a great 'at and feathers like a 'Ighlander's, and never answering no more nor a stuffed himage!

FATHER (*to the Husband of* THE OWNER OF THE HAT). Will you tell your good lady to take her 'at off, Sir, please?

THE OWNER OF THE HAT (*to her Husband*). Don't you do nothing of the sort, Sam, or you'll 'ear of it!

THE MOTHER. Some people are perlite, I must say. Parties might *beyave* as ladies when they come in the Pit! It's a pity her 'usband can't teach her better manners!

THE FATHER. '*Im* teach her! 'E knows better. 'E's got a Tartar there, '*e* 'as!

THE OWNER OF THE HAT. Sam, are you going to set by and hear me insulted like this?

HER HUSBAND (*turning round tremulously*). I—I'll trouble you to drop making these personal allusions to my wife's 'at, Sir. It's puffickly impossible to listen to what's going on on the stage with all these remarks be'ind!

THE FATHER. Not more nor it is to *see* what's going on on the stage with that 'at in front! I paid 'arf-a-crown to see the Pantermime, I did; not to 'ave a view of your wife's 'at! . . . 'Ere, Maria, blowed if I can stand this 'ere game any longer. Jimmy must change places again, and if he can't see, he must jest stand up on the seat, that's all!

[JIMMY *is transferred to his original place, and mounts upon the seat.*

A PITTITE BEHIND JIMMY (*touching up* JIMMY'S *Father with an umbrella*). Will you tell your little boy to set down, please, and not block the view like this?

JIMMY'S FATHER. If you can indooce that lady in front to take off her 'at, I will—but not before. Stay where you are, Jimmy, my boy.

THE PITTITE BEHIND. Well, I must stand myself then, that's all. I mean to see, *somehow*! [*He rises.*

PEOPLE BEHIND HIM (*sternly*). Set down there, will yer?
[*He resumes his seat expostulating.*

JIMMY. Father, the gentleman behind is a pinching of my legs!

JIMMY'S FATHER. Will you stop pinching my little boy's legs! He ain't doing *you* no 'arm—is he?

THE PINCHING PITTITE. Let him sit down, then!

JIMMY'S FATHER. Let the lady take her 'at off!

MURMURS BEHIND. Order, there! Set down! Put that boy down! Take orf that 'at! Silence in front, there! Turn 'em out! Shame! . . . &c., &c.

THE HUSBAND OF THE O. OF THE H. (*in a whisper to his Wife*). Take off the blessed 'at, and have done with it, do!

THE O. OF THE H. What—*now!* I'd sooner *die* in the 'at!

[*An* ATTENDANT *is called.*

THE ATTENDANT. Order, there, Gentlemen, please—unless you want to get turned out! No standing allowed on the seats—you're disturbing the performance 'ere, you know!

[JIMMY *is made to sit down, and weeps silently; the hubbub gradually subsides—and* THE OWNER OF THE HAT *triumphs —for the moment.*

JIMMY'S MOTHER. Never mind, my boy, you shall have Mother's seat in a minute. I dessay, if all was known, the lady 'as reasons for keeping her 'at on, pore thing!

THE FATHER (*perceiving her drift*). Ah, I never thought o' that. So she may. Very likely her 'at won't *come* off—not without her '*air!*

THE MOTHER. Ah, well, we mustn't be 'ard on her, if that's so.

THE O. OF THE H. (*removing the obstruction*). I 'ope you're satisfied *now*, I'm sure?

THE FATHER (*handsomely*). Better late nor never, Mum, and we take it kind of you. Though, why you shouldn't ha' done it at fust, I dunno; for you look a deal 'ansomer without the 'at than what you did in it— *don't* she, Maria?

THE O. OF THE H. (*mollified*). Sam, ask the gentleman behind if his little boy would like a ginger-nut.

[*This olive-branch is accepted; compliments pass; cordiality is re-stored, and the Pantomime proceeds without further disturbance.*

RICHARD CLAY AND SONS, LIMITED, LONDON AND BUNGAY.